D1041568

and a body
to remember with

Carmen Rodríguez

ARSENAL PULP PRESS
Vancouver

ARSENAL PULP PRESS
103-1014 Homer Street
Vancouver, B.C.
Canada V6B 2W9

The publisher gratefully acknowledges the support of the Canada Council for the Arts for its publishing program, and the support of the Book Publishing Industry Development Program, and the B.C. Arts Council.

The following stories were previously published: "accented living" and "in the company of words" (*Aquelarre*); "adios piazzolla" (*The Malahat Review*); "trespass" (*West Coast Line*); "the mirror" (*Prison Journal*); "breaking the ice" (*Possibilitiis*); "the labyrinths of love" (*The Antigonish Review*); "a balanced diet: laughing and crying at the house in the air" (*Descant*); "hands" (*The Capilano Review*).

The line "*Gracias a la vida que me ha dado tanto*" ("Thanks to life that has given me so much") in "i sing, therefore i am" is from *Gracias a la Vida*, a song by Chilean composer and artist Violeta Parra.

Typeset by the Vancouver Desktop Publishing Centre
Printed and bound in Canada

CANADIAN CATALOGUING IN PUBLICATION DATA:

Rodríguez, Carmen, 1948-
    And a body to remember with

ISBN 1-55125-044-3

    I. Title.
PS8585.O373A72 1997   C813'.54   C97-910743-1
PR9199.3.R5428A72 1997

CONTENTS

Fragments of memory. But the brevity,
like a gasp of air quickly held, the
body slow to let go.

—LYDIA KWA,
The Colours of Heroines

Tal vez, tal vez el olvido sobre la tierra como una copa
puede desarrollar el crecimiento y alimentar la vida
(puede ser), como el humus sombrío en el bosque.
. . .
Tal vez, pero mi plato es otro, mi alimento es distinto:
mis ojos no vinieron para morder olvido:
mis labios se abren sobre todo el tiempo, y todo el tiempo,
no sólo una parte del tiempo ha gastado mis manos.

Por eso te hablaré de estos dolores que quisiera apartar,
te obligaré a vivir una vez más entre sus quemaduras,
no para detenernos como en una estación, al partir,
ni tampoco para golpear con la frente la tierra,
ni para llenarnos el corazón con agua salada,
sino para caminar conociendo, para tocar la rectitud
con decisiones infinitamente cargadas de sentido,
para que la severidad sea una condición de la alegría, para
que así seamos invencibles.

Perhaps, perhaps oblivion can foster growth and feed life
on the earth, like a cupola
(maybe), like dark humus in the forest.
. . .
Perhaps, but my plate is another one, my food is different:
my eyes did not come to bite on oblivion:
my lips are open upon all times, and all the time,
not only one part of time has weathered my hands.

That's why I will speak to you about those pains that
          I would like to push aside,
I will force you to live once again in their burning wounds,
not so that we can linger as if at a station, when departing,
or pound the earth with our forehead.
Not so that we can fill our heart with salty water,
but so that we can walk knowingly, touch rectitude
with decisions infinitely loaded with meaning.
So that severity can become a condition for joy, so that
we can become invincible.

                        —PABLO NERUDA,
                          Canto General/General Song

ACKNOWLEDGEMENTS

I AM GRATEFUL TO Nancy Richler, Lydia Kwa, and Angela Hryniuk for their friendship. Without their encouragement, I would have never believed that I was capable of writing in English. I also thank them for reading the manuscript and providing invaluable feedback.

My son Ted (Lalo) Everton and daughters Carmen and Alejandra Aguirre nourished me with their love and support throughout the process of writing *and a body to remember with*. Lalo acted as my "junior" editor by providing feedback on linguistic matters. Alejandra took the photograph for the cover of the Spanish version of the book and Carmen posed for the photograph.

A grant from the Canada Council allowed me to dedicate myself to completing the manuscript. I thank them for their financial support.

And finally, I thank Alan Creighton-Kelly, not only for the picture, but for everything.

FOREWORD

THESE SHORT STORIES ARE THE PRODUCT of not only a long and intense creative process, but also of an interesting linguistic exercise. Most of them, or at least most parts of them, were originally written in Spanish, my mother tongue. Until a few years ago, I sought the help of translators to take them from Spanish into English. In fact, earlier versions of a few of these stories, or parts of them, were translated by Lori Nordstrom, Heidi Neufeld Raine, and Helen Dixon.

However, in the last four or five years, with the encouragement of my friends, the writers Nancy Richler, Lydia Kwa, and Angela Hryniuk, I began the fascinating process of translating them myself. But it only took a few attempts to realize that I had embarked on something that could no longer be called "translation." As I looked for the best English words and constructions to do justice to the initial Spanish text, new associations and feelings came to mind. As a consequence, the English versions departed from the original and developed into something quite different. Then I realized that I would have to "translate" the new versions back into Spanish. But again, as I did that, new words made their way into the manuscript. Back and forth I went, many times, until I felt that both tips of my tongue and my two sets of ears were satisfied with the final product.

In many ways, this process mirrors my hyphenated existence. I live and work on a teeter-totter, moving back and forth between two cultures and languages. In a paper that I read at the Writing Thru Race conference (Vancouver, 1994) and that was later published by Sister Vision Press in *The Other Woman: Women of Colour in Contemporary Canadian Literature* (edited by Makeda Silvera, 1994), I stated: "For me, living and writing in a hyphen implies translation. . . . [It] is important to use the hyphen of my bilingualism, my biculturalism, the hyphen of my double identity as a bridge, so at least I can invite other Canadians to read my work. I want Canadians to read my work. I have so much to tell!"

Working through this collection, I have realized that what I have to tell is not only in the content of the stories themselves, but also in the process of their bilingual, bicultural creation. I live, struggle, and work here, but I cannot forget where I came from. My heart trespasses borders and stretches over a whole continent to find its home at the two extremes of the Americas: in Chile and in Canada. And my hand writes in two languages: Spanish, my mother tongue, and English, my adopted tongue.

I am a Chilean-Canadian writer.

—CARMEN RODRÍGUEZ

To the memory of Nelson Rodríguez, brother and compañero, because he lived in the burning wounds.

To the memory of Carmen Cortés, mother and compañera, because she never forgot.

Y también para Ana María, Coto y Manelo.

black hole

THE PROBLEM ESTELA DE RAMÍREZ HAD when she arrived in Canada was that she had nothing to hold on to. At most, some pictures in an issue of *National Geographic* from who-knows-when, showing snow-capped mountains and crystal-blue lakes with a hotel that looked like a castle—or maybe she was getting confused and the pictures were from Switzerland. . . .

It wasn't as if she had been told, Look, Estela, tomorrow you're going to Buenos Aires. If she had been told Buenos Aires, Estela would've thought of Evita Perón, the River Plate, a good barbecue, the line "It was raining, was raining," the way Leonardo Favio sang it in that deep, masculine voice. . . . Or she would've started to hum a tango and told herself things like, I'm going to go to Corrientes Street and see what's at Number 348, or tomorrow I'm going to see Florida Street and the Obelisco. The point is that she would've thought of something.

Even if she had been told, Look, Estela, tomorrow you're going to England, she would've thought of Queen Elizabeth in a pale blue low-cut dress, drinking tea with her little finger poised, like she was in that magazine *Para Ti*, and she would've remembered her mom saying, Look how bad things must be if now even the Queen is baring her breasts.

But when Estela de Ramírez was told that tomorrow she was going to Canada, nothing came to her mind. Canada. And when her daughters asked her, Mom, Mom, what's Canada like? all Estela de Ramírez told them was, It's a very big country at the other end of the world. If she started to tell them that it had mountains and lakes and snow, the girls might get all excited and now that she thought about it, those *National Geographic* pictures were probably of Switzerland. . . . Now, girls, she told them, I have a lot of things to do, so go ask your dad. And only then she remembered that the girls couldn't go ask their dad because their dad was in jail and tomorrow, after ten months, they were going to see him for the first time on the plane to Canada. Estela de Ramírez couldn't think of anything better to do than to cry, the kind of crying that sounds like part hiccup and part laughing attack. Then the girls started to cry just like their mother, and the three of them cried and cried, sitting on their suitcases, surrounded by chaos and echoes in their house of Catedral Abajo, in the *barrio* Quinta Normal, their heads filled with a hole called Canada.

The three cried again when the girls' grandmother took out her white handkerchief and began to wave it and to throw kisses as they climbed the stairway to the plane, the girls in their white organdy dresses and patent leather shoes, and Estela de Ramírez in her tailored suit and black heels. They cried even more when they saw Manuel Ramírez, thin and wasted, but neat, and with a big smile, sitting in 20C of the Canadian Pacific Airlines economy class, handcuffed to the seat.

His handcuffs were removed just before the plane took off, and for the first time since the night of October 2nd, 1973, Manuel Ramírez was able to hug his family. The girls climbed all over him and Estela couldn't stop kissing his face and his neck. She would've even climbed on top of him, in spite of the suit, the black heels, the wrinkled nose of the woman in 21C and the man who kept clearing his throat in 20D, but the stewardess announced that everybody had to remain seated and fasten their seat belts because the plane was taking off. A miniature Santiago disappeared beneath the clouds while the hole called Canada began to take possession of Estela de Ramírez's stomach, chest, throat, head, ears, and mouth.

This became evident when they arrived in Vancouver and Estela realized that when she opened her mouth, nothing would come out, not even the "This is a table and that's a chair" that Miss Soto had taught her in *Liceo #2*. As well, she didn't understand shit about what people said. At least she was happy that Vancouver did have snow-capped mountains and lots of water. But the more she thought about it, the more it seemed to her that those pictures in the *National Geographic* were of Switzerland. . . .

The first few days at the Ace Motor Hotel were very, very strange: interminable hallways covered in red and black carpets, the smell of sweaty feet mixed with french fries, and doors on both sides opening from time to time, exposing inscrutable faces and sounds from who-knows-what latitudes. Their room, paid for by the Department of Immigration, had two large beds, one for the couple and one for the girls. But every night they all ended up huddled together in one bed, shivering with cold, even though by now they knew that in Vancouver, August is the height of summer.

After one week, Estela de Ramírez already knew a few things about Canada: that the post office was around the corner and that letters to Chile cost twenty-three cents. That the letter carrier arrived at the hotel at about eleven each morning, and that all those inscrutable faces in the hallway would gather at the hotel door and throw themselves on the poor man until the desk-clerk would yell like a madman, grabbing all the letters and handing them out as if he were Santa Claus. That when anyone looked at her and seemed to be speaking to her, she could say "No speak English" and they would leave her alone. That in Vancouver there was no public square and therefore, no band that played at noon on Sundays. That Vancouver beaches had no waves. That the Chilean coast was more beautiful. That the mountains in Vancouver were quite big and lovely. That the Andes were bigger and more lovely.

Those first weeks in Canada, Estela de Ramírez began to dream the same dream every night: her Aunt Lina, the one who had the accident the year before, was sitting in the front seat of the Castillo Velasco bus when, out of the corner of her eye, she saw a huge truck coming at them at full speed. Aunt Lina screamed and closed her eyes, and when she opened them, Estela de Ramírez knew that it wasn't Aunt Lina who had been sitting in the front seat of the Castillo Velasco bus, but she, Estela, falling now with the bus and everything else into a black hole called Canada, with nothing to hold on to, not a bosom, not a melody or the name of a street, nothing, not even the pictures in the *National Geographic* from who-knows-when, showing mountains, lakes and snow, because now, as she fell, she remembered that the pictures were of Switzerland. Now she was absolutely sure that they were not of Canada.

Vancouver, April 19, 1980

Dearest *Mami*:

How's everybody doing? Got your letter about a week ago, guess it only took about five days to get here. Not bad, eh? I still

find it hard to believe that you're in fall while we are in spring.
The weather has been great and the city looks beautiful with its
snow-capped mountains, the sky so blue, lots of sailboats out in
the ocean and block after block of cherry trees in bloom. I love
taking the girls to Stanley Park on Sundays and showing them
all the flowers. The tulips are particularly impressive. I always
thought that tulips were sort of Holland's national flowers,
right? Well, at least that's what the magazines would lead you to
believe. But they grow here too and I doubt that Holland's tulips
would be any more beautiful than ours.

We're doing really well. Manuel is as happy as a little boy in a
toy store. Setting up his own shop was definitely the best thing
he could do. He's such a good mechanic that it's taken him no
time to build a steady clientele, so we've had no problem making
the loan payments every month. Did I tell you the name of the
shop? It's called *El Cóndor* and the logo shows a white-collared
black condor, with his wings spread out, flying over the Andes.
Our friend Toya, the one that I've told you about, the one that
used to work as a kids' book illustrator for Quimantú, designed
it and also painted the sign. We'll send you a picture as soon as
we can. The girls are also very happy and proud of their dad.
They love going to visit him in the shop and they want to know
everything about every tool, every client, every car. Who knows,
maybe they'll be mechanics when they grow up!

Manuel wants me to quit my job and help him at the shop
with the paperwork and stuff, but no way José. I love my work
and I didn't go to college for two years to end up shuffling papers
at my husband's shop, don't you think? He says that I would
have a lot less stress, but what he doesn't understand is that I
love working with children and that I wouldn't give up my
monthly paycheque for anything. Anyway, I just feel frustrated
with him sometimes. The only reason he agreed to me going to

school and working in the first place was because of the money situation. So now he thinks that because he can support the family without my help, I should just leave the daycare and help *him* with his work!

The girls are growing like weeds and, in my eyes, they are becoming more and more beautiful as time goes by. But I'm sort of sad because Natalia doesn't want her braids anymore and she's been bugging me to take her to get her hair cut. What do you think? She's got such beautiful thick hair that it would be a crime to chop it off. And little Panchi, the copycat, now she's saying that she wants her hair cut too! I don't know what to do.

Three days ago Panchi came home crying and I couldn't get her to stop or tell me what the matter was. Finally she blurted out that she hated me, she hated her dad and everybody in the family because we are dark-skinned and have black hair and brown eyes and that's why she's the same way. Listen to this: she wants to be white and have blonde hair and blue eyes! Can you imagine? I almost had a heart attack. I was so shocked that at first I didn't know what to do, I just looked at her with my mouth open and couldn't say anything. Then I picked her up, took her to the bathroom, and made her look at herself in the mirror. I made her tell me what colour her skin was, her hair and her eyes. It took her quite a while to answer, and you should've heard the contempt in her voice. After each one of her responses I said: yes, that's right, you are dark because you are Chilean, and you are beautiful. Do you hear me? You are beautiful!

I don't know if I did the right thing, but I still get this pain in my chest when I remember the look in her eyes, full of hurt and hatred for me and herself. After a while, she broke down and cried in my arms for a long time. Yes, Mom, I cried with her too, in spite of you telling me that I have to be strong and not cry in front of the girls. But I was so devastated I couldn't help it. She has looked happy and carefree in the last couple of days, so I hope she's okay. It'll take a while for me to feel okay.

Anyway, this is starting to read like a novel instead of a letter. It's late and I have the early shift tomorrow, so I have to get up at six. I know that's no big deal for you, but for me it is, so I'd better say 'bye. Tell that brother of mine to write or at least send a card once in a while. Say hi to Aunt Lina, *doña* Olvido, Mr. Orozco, and Gino. How is Aunt Lina's health? I get very homesick when I think of all of you and our *barrio*, particularly now that it's fall and the trees on the Quinta Normal are shedding their crunchy leaves. I'll probably have a dream about that tonight.

Write soon. Hugs and kisses from your son in-law and your granddaughters. A special bear hug and many kisses from me, your daughter,

Estela

P.S. The girls drew pictures of Stanley Park to send you. Aren't they cute?

July 1, 1980
Hello, yes, operator, a long-distance call to Chile, please . . . yes, Santiago . . . seven three five one four . . . yes, five digits only . . . okay, thank you. . . . *Mami*, Mom, hi, it's me. . . . No, no, everything is okay. . . . Yes, everybody's fine. . . . The girls, too. . . . Yes, Manuel is finishing a job at the shop. . . . Yes, it's going very well. . . . Tell me about you, how are you? . . . Good, and Renato? . . . Well, Mom, you know what he's like. . . . But Mom, you can't control his life anymore, you know, he's an adult. . . . Yes, I know he lives at home, but. . . . Anyway, Mom, listen. . . .

We became Canadian citizens today. . . . Come on, Mom, don't be like that. . . . No, there's no reason to feel like that. . . . We live here, you know. . . . Well, of course, some time, but you know that we're not allowed to even go visit now. . . . Why do you think I hadn't told you before? Because of this, because I knew you would make a scene and try to stop us from doing it, that's why. . . . Mom, you don't stop being who you are because you become a Canadian citizen, you know. . . . Besides, now you can come and stay with us, now that we're citizens. . . . Well, Mom, I'm not saying that you should stay forever. . . . Yeah, a few months at least. . . . It's expensive and it's a long trip. . . . You know that we want you to come. . . . The girls are all excited. . . . Yeah, they were very proud to become Canadian citizens. . . . Yes, Mother. . . . Yes, I did talk to them about being Chilean. . . . Yes. . . . Well, now they say they are Chilean-Canadian. . . . No, she hasn't said anything about wanting to be blonde anymore. . . . Yes, they both have short hair now. . . . Looks good. . . . They love it. . . . It's okay, Mom. . . . We have to adapt and accept things, you know. . . . How do I feel? Fine, I guess. . . . Yeah, it makes me sad, but part of me also feels proud. . . . Oh, Mom, come on, why do you ask me if you can't take my answer? . . . Mom, please don't cry. . . . I haven't forgotten my origins and my history, Mom. . . . It doesn't have to be black-and-white, you know. . . . Mom, it's *not* black-and-white. . . . Yes, it took a long time but I do like it here. . . . I like it there too, of course. . . . Yes, Mom, one day we will go back. . . . Do you think I would find work at a daycare centre? . . . That's an idea. . . . Yeah, a bilingual daycare centre. . . . But Mom, this doesn't make any sense, we'll think about it when the time comes. . . . Yes, I guess he could take all his equipment. . . . Why are you talking about this? You know that we can't go back, we've just become Canadian citizens. . . . We live here, this is where our lives are. . . .

Listen, please listen. . . . Okay, we would like you to come up, remember? . . . Good. . . . What about for Christmas? . . . Well, it will probably take a while for the paper work. . . . Yes, I will send you everything by courier so it doesn't get lost. . . . I know it's expensive but we don't want the papers to get lost, right? . . . Yes, there's stuff you have to do there at the Embassy. . . . We have to do stuff here too. . . . Of course we will send you the ticket. . . . As soon as we find out exactly what we have to do. . . . Okay, listen, this is turning out to be very expensive. . . . Okay, so you'll get the papers soon, okay? . . . Yes, I'll write too. . . . Thank you, I thought you would never say "Congratulations." . . . Yes, I know you feel like giving us your condolences. . . . Come on Mom, it's okay, don't worry about it. . . . He's fine with it. . . . It's good for his business too, you know? . . . Okay, we've gotta say 'bye now. . . . Mom, can't I tell you about that in a letter? . . . Okay, quickly then, the girls wore red and white cotton dresses and sandals and I wore a blue silk dress. . . . Mom, how could they wear their organdy dresses? . . . They're six years older now! . . . Mom. . . . Yes, I did keep them. . . . No, they don't like patent leather shoes anymore. . . . No, no socks. . . . It's summertime here. . . . Yes, red high heels. . . . Red. . . . A suit and a tie. . . . I knew you would like that. . . . Okay, Mom, gotta go. . . . Yes, love you too. . . . Okay, I will. . . . Love to everybody there. . . . Okay, talk to you soon. . . . *Chao*. . . .

Santiago, February 19, 1981

My dearest daughter,
You probably believe I'm an ingrate, leaving Vancouver so abruptly, but I don't know, *mijita*, I was feeling like a prisoner, couldn't speak to anybody, not even to my granddaughters,

couldn't go for my daily shopping, everything so different, do you know what I mean?

I also felt very sad to see how different you all are, the girls didn't even like my cooking anymore, all they want is that hamburger garbage. . . . I think that's bad for them, Estela, you shouldn't let them eat only what they like, it's not good for their health. Don't you cook *cazuela* or *salpicón* anymore? They are good, hearty dishes, *mija*, you should try to get the girls to eat them.

Your house is very nice, but you know that I've never liked electric stoves, at least with gas stoves you see the flame, you know. It was so hard to cook on that stove, everything seemed to turn out tasteless. Maybe it was just my imagination, but I couldn't feel comfortable cooking on that stove. Also, I've been thinking that wall-to-wall carpeting cannot be good, *mija*, all that dust that accumulates and besides, the carpet could become a breeding nest for who-knows-what kind of bugs. I think you should look into it.

Daughter, I'm very proud of you, the way you speak English so well, how you drive your own car and you have your own job and everything, but don't you think the girls and Manuel need you at home? Now that he has his shop and can make good money, perhaps you could just relax a little bit and help him out. You are always so busy, running everywhere, and then doing the housework, it's too much for one person, you know. Think about it, Estelita, think of your health, your daughters will need you for many more years to come.

Anyway, everybody here was surprised to see me back so soon, they think that Canada is like a paradise, can't understand why I didn't want to stay. I feel very sad inside, people don't know the meaning of the word "exile." Manuel's hair, completely grey and the pain in your eyes, daughter, I didn't want to say anything when I was there, but I can't keep it in any longer. The pain in your eyes really haunts me. You look so good but your eyes look so sad. I know you, Estela, you are my child, and I know that something inside you has died.

Oh my God, it's so difficult not to hate those military bastards when you have so much pain pent up inside, a whole generation being brought up in other countries, with other values, in other languages. My two darling granddaughters don't want to speak Spanish anymore, not even to their own grandmother, and they're growing up without their grandparents, uncles, and aunts. I'm sure you know all this, daughter, but now I know it too, I know what it means. When I fell in love with your father, when I had you and Renato, when your father died, when my granddaughters were born, I never ever thought that our family would be separated like this. Oh God, it's so difficult not to hate the bastards. So much pain. So much.

Estelita, I don't even know if I'll send you this letter, perhaps it's better that I don't, but I also feel the need to tell you how I feel. I was so happy when I was young, I loved riding my bicycle, I laughed all the time, I did everything my mother told me to as long as she gave me permission to ride my bike. But life is so hard, it hardens you up, it makes you mean. I was able to bring Renato and you up basically on my own, after your father's fatal heart attack (may he rest in peace), but I never thought that we would end up at the two extremes of the world.

I guess I have to be grateful that we are all alive and well. Yes, I am grateful. Yes, I feel better now, *mija*. I'm so sorry I couldn't stay longer to help you and to be with you. You know that I love you, Manuel and the girls so much. I don't know what happened to me.

Lina is doing fine, same thing with everybody else in the neighbourhood. Renato kept the house fairly clean while I was away. He even remembered to water the plants!

Please write soon. I already put the Christmas pictures in an album and I have it on the coffee table for everybody to see. They all think you guys look great. People can't believe how tall the girls are. Daughter, forgive me for not being able to stay longer. I hope you'll understand. Hugs and kisses to Natalia, Panchi, Manuel, and all the Chileans I met there. Also to Linda, your neighbour. Too bad I couldn't talk to her. A big hug for you, my sweet daughter. Your mother,

Maura

P.S. I looked in the boxes that you left behind but I couldn't find that *National Geographic* you asked me for. They seem to have articles about all the countries in the world, except for Canada. Anyway, I'll look again in case I missed it.

April 23, 1987
Hello . . . hello . . . Natalia, is that you? . . . Yes, your *abuelita* . . . your grandma . . . yes . . . from Santiago, of course. . . . I said Santiago, of course. . . . You sound like a young woman, Natalita. . . . I said you sound like a young woman. . . . Doesn't matter. . . . Is your Mom there? . . . Yes . . . your Mom. . . . Hello, Estela? . . . Hi, daughter, how are you all? . . . Yes, fine. . . . Fine, too. . . . Natalia sounds so grown up. . . . Of course I know she'll be seventeen this year. . . . Estela, Estelita, listen to me, I'm so excited. . . . Well, listen, I have great news for you and Manuel. . . . You're off the blacklist! . . . I said you're off the blacklist! . . . Yes, of course I'm sure! . . . It's in today's paper, Estela! They published the names of all the people who are off the blacklist as of today. . . . Yes. . . . Now you guys can come back! . . . I've got it right here, Estela, listen. . . . Number 2,637:

Ramírez Esquivel Manuel Armando . . . and you . . . let's see, I marked the paper . . . here it is . . . your maiden name . . . Number 865: González Reyes Estela del Carmen . . . Estela . . . Estelita. . . . Say something, for Christ's sake! . . . Aren't you excited? . . . Oh, my sweetheart, are you crying? . . . Oh, don't cry, my love. . . . Oh, I wish I could cuddle you in my arms like when you were little. . . . Yes, my love, you can come back to your country now, after thirteen years in exile, you can come back. . . . Well, it was because of the fuss over the Pope's visit. . . . Yeah, apparently they were told to clean up their human rights act if they wanted the Pope to visit. . . . Yeah, they released some political prisoners too. . . . Well, that's what the paper says. . . . *La Tercera*. . . . Of course it's accurate, Estela. Lina told me she read it in *El Mercurio* too. It's all over the news. On TV too. . . . Yeah. . . . Everybody's here. . . . Well, everybody came to visit. . . . Yeah, everybody's excited. . . . Well, Lina's here, and *Señora* Olvido, and Renato, of course, and Gino. . . . *Señor* Orozco is coming in a little while. . . . Well, they just wanted to celebrate with me. . . . Yeah, I made a little cake. . . . Is Manuel back from work? . . . Okay, yes. . . . Manuel? Manuel? Is that you? . . . Fine, dear. . . . Isn't this fantastic news? . . . Today, just today. . . . Lina phoned me to tell me and then Gino showed up with *La Tercera* . . . and it was on the news on TV at noon, and . . . yes, any time you want. . . . Listen, Lina brought some champagne, listen to the cork. . . . Did you hear? Get Estela on the other phone. . . . Now we're going to toast. . . . *Salud . . . salud por el retorno* . . . Did you hear everybody? . . . Yes, everybody is very happy for you. . . . So, when do you think you can come? I could find out things for you guys. . . . Good mechanics are needed everywhere, you know. . . . Of course, I understand. . . . Yeah, and Estelita, you could have your own bilingual daycare centre. . . . Yes, daughter. . . . Everybody's going nuts here. . . . Well, think about it, of course. . . . Let me know when you're coming, then. . . . I understand, I understand. . . . You know that you can stay here for as long as you need to. . . . Well, just so that you know. . . . Okay, Manuel. . . . Estela, daughter, say hello to Panchi for me as well. . . . I wonder how the girls will take the news. . . . Yes, we'll see. . . . Yes, of course, no rush. . . . You're right. . . . Okay, everybody sends their love. . . . Can you hear them? . . . Okay. . . . I still can't believe it, can you? . . . All right, take care. . . . Yes, I will. . . . Love you too, sweetheart. . . . Congratulations. . . . Well, because now you can come back! . . . Yes, congratulations to you too, Manuel. . . . Love to everybody. . . . *Chao.* . . . *Chao.* . . .

When Estela de Ramírez was told that she could go back to Chile, she was invaded by a mixture of excitement and terror, anxiety and nostalgia. The daily crying fits began the same evening that her mother called. She cried for hours on her husband's shoulder, before the alarmed eyes of her daughters, who didn't know what to do to comfort her.

That night she dreamed that she was walking around the Santiago *Plaza de Armas*, dressed in a slip, holding hands with her mother, while they listened to the *Carabineros* wind ensemble, one Sunday at noon. The plaza was full of people displaying their best dresses, boys in white shirts and flannel pants, gelled forelocks and polished shoes, girls in organdy dresses and patent leather shoes, butterfly bows in their hair. Estela seemed to recognize people she had known a long time ago, but when she approached them to say hello, she realized that she had made a mistake, and actually, no, that was not *Señora* Margarita, the owner of the Río Claro vegetable shop, and that one was not Ramona, her grade nine classmate.

She thought that the eleven o'clock mass at the Metropolitan Cathedral would be over anytime now and yes, she would be able to greet some people she knew. But when she looked across the street, instead of seeing the Santiago Cathedral, she saw the Vancouver City Hall building, its clock showing twelve noon, the garden covered with tulips. Estela felt a strange sort of excitement and turned her face to say to her mother, Look, *Mami*, that's the Vancouver City Hall building, but her *mami* was not beside her anymore and the warmth in her hand was actually the hand of a military man, walking absent-mindedly beside her. She woke up crying and Manuel Ramírez had to rock her like a baby for the rest of the night.

During the day, while she played with the children at the daycare centre or drove in the Vancouver traffic, she made efforts to remember places, faces, smells, colours, accents, but she could never achieve the clarity that she was looking for. Everything appeared blurred, pale, distorted. When she thought, Yes, now I remember what Monjitas Street looked like, she realized that she wasn't sure whether that café was indeed there, or on Main Street. When she tried to find in her memory the appetizing aroma of a Chilean *asado*, the smell of Burger King hamburgers took over. When she thought that now she had finally found the face of Miss Soto, her English teacher at the *Liceo #2*, Mrs. Cheung, her supervisor at the daycare centre, showed up with her long, pointy nose.

Those first few weeks after the call, Estela lived in a thick fog. As usual, Manuel Ramírez left for the shop early in the morning, but did not come home until late, claiming he had tons of work. Every evening, Estela waited for him with *cazuela, charquicán,*

salpicón, pancutras, chupe de queso, pastel de choclo, and all those
dishes that she had forgotten about thirteen years earlier. The
day after the call, she had looked for Laura Amenábar's recipe
book, *Para Saber Cocinar*, which she had brought from Chile
and buried in a box as soon as she had arrived in Canada. She
copied the list of ingredients on a slip of paper and after work
she went to the supermarket to buy what she needed. She had
also found the few cassettes of Chilean music she had packed in
her suitcase that last night in her Santiago house of Catedral
Abajo. Now, every evening, she locked herself up in the kitchen
to listen to the forgotten songs, prepare the old recipes, and cry
her eyes out.

Natalia and Panchi stopped asking their friends over because
their mother wouldn't let them listen to rock music at full blast
as they were used to, served them the unbearable dishes that their
grandmother had made, and refused to speak to them in English.
Estela de Ramírez didn't realize that her daughters didn't understand a word of what she was saying, and that they left the dishes
of food intact on the table, and were obviously losing weight.
She herself began to put on weight, because she not only ate what
was on her own plate, but absent- mindedly devoured what her
daughters didn't. After dinner, she would sit like a zombie in
front of the TV and when Manuel Ramírez got home from the
shop, she served him his dinner and helped herself to another
plate as well.

The dreams in which Chilean and Canadian scenes blurred
together were repeated every night. Stanley Park would show up
by the ocean in Viña del Mar, or the Alameda would replace
Burrard Street in downtown Vancouver. In all of those dreams
she would wander around as a semi-naked ghost, not recognized
by anybody and not recognizing anybody herself.

And then one night the black holes appeared. She began to

have the same dream every night: she was walking along the seawall in English Bay covered with a sheet (only that the seawall went around the Cerro Santa Lucía and Miraflores Street had become a fast-flowing river), when in the middle of the walkway a big dark blotch appeared. Estela approached it cautiously and looked at it with curious eyes. There was nothing there. Only blackness. She tried to go around the hole to continue walking, but the hole grew bigger and bigger. She thought of jumping over to the other side, but the hole grew even larger. She decided to walk back, but when she turned around, another black hole had appeared behind her. She looked around for something to hold on to, maybe a tree, a flower, another human being, but everything had turned black.

Estela de Ramírez felt the cement break with the sound of loud thunder under her feet. She fell into the abyss with nothing to hold on to, not a face, not a tulip, not a mountain, because the fleeting images that came to her mind instantly became blurred and turned into more and more blackness. She screamed, desperately, her arms outstretched, her hands extended. When she realized that she was surrounded by nothingness, she wanted to hug her own body, only now she realized that her body was the hole and the hole was her. The only clear thing in the midst of total darknesss was her voice, trapped in her throat, trying to remember how to cry out for help . . . but, in what language?

the mirror

In the morning, at breakfast,
while things slowly awaken,
I will call you by my name
and you will answer
joyfully,
my equal, my sister, my fellow woman.
                    —CRISTINA PERI ROSSI

I NEVER KNEW YOUR REAL NAME. You were Cristina and you'll stay Cristina in my memory; Cristina, fragile form, Cristina, faltering breath, Cristina, child's face with huge, frightened eyes.

It was said that there were terrorists, that they were heartless, relentless. It was also said that the military tortured people; so many things were said. . . . You know very well that I don't condone violence of any kind, no matter how justifiable it may seem—how often we discussed it! But when Juanita and Miguel asked whether I'd take you in, I had to accept. They said you were dying. Everything imaginable had been done to you, as well as everything unimaginable. It never occurred to me that there would be doctors right there, during the sessions themselves, to stop the torturer at the crucial instant, that fragile line that separates life from death.

In the theatre, I often had to act out that very moment. I had to review my own life, blended with the life of my character, to arrive at the moment when the spirit separates from the body and floats away. How often I lived it on stage! . . . to such an extent that I had to use all my strength to go back again and continue living as myself, as Clara.

And you were there, in that suspended state, not on stage, but in a torture chamber. They had put you there, the target of a sick violence that had been contrived and designed, studied and put into practice by minds and hands like those of any other human being—hands like these that took you in, that cold August night.

They told me they'd bring you at dawn, if everything went well. They had a scheme to get you out of prison. Your heart had just about given out and your surface wounds were starting to get infected. I don't know how important you were to your organization; I don't know why this impressive deployment of lives to save yours. All I know is that to me, all human life deserves the highest respect. Even the lives of inhuman people, people who behave inhumanely, like your torturers, deserve respect. And your *compañeros* decided to risk their lives to save yours.

Your *compañeros*, as you called them, and even I came to call them: your *compañeros*—my only family, you told me one day. Yes, you would've liked to have children and go to dinner at your parents' house on Sundays. That's the fantasy of every woman of the revolution, you said. And sure, as an actress with an impressive career behind me, I knew these fantasies well. I had made the decision a long time ago to be a single woman, and of course I fantasized about children coming home from school and Sunday *empanadas*. But no man I knew had wanted to be Clara's partner. Clara, who was stopped for autographs when she went shopping. Clara, who went out every afternoon to work and didn't come back until after midnight. Clara, who really couldn't (didn't want to?) take on the responsibilities which are so traditionally a woman's in a relationship.

That August night I waited for you like a girl of fourteen waiting to make love for the first time in her life. I didn't know if you'd hurt me, if I'd like you, or if I'd feel used and then discarded. I only knew that I'd agreed and that it was already too late to take it back. With the lights out, I ruined the manicure they'd given me that afternoon in the theatre and damned myself a thousand times for my obsession with risking everything for an act of love that would surely do me more harm than good.

It was a spooky arrival; I had to hold myself back to keep from shouting against the invasion. Barely visible in the semi-darkness of dawn was a silhouette, wrapped in a too-big coat, feet dragging between Juanita and Miguel. The pale face almost glowed in the gloom of the hallway . . . and the eyes, the eyes! What I wouldn't have given to be able to achieve that expression combining fear and absolute fatigue!

In the light of day, your wounds took on a life and movement of their own. For the neighbours, the doctor became my lover and his daily visit was decorated with bouquets of roses and gladioli. I became used to greeting him in the doorway with open arms. I knew that at eleven each morning, all the curtains on the block would part halfway to enjoy the rendezvous. We made you comfortable in bed, and I held your head and your hand as he attacked the beaten skin.

Your eyes looked at me with a dampness I hated because, what did I have to do with your eyes, your sores, your dry, clenched mouth? What did I have to do with your stifled cries and grotesque contortions? Oh, how I hated your wounds, your pain. Why had I done this to myself? Why had I brought a stranger into my home? Didn't I have enough with my own pain?

But love grew. At the beginning, you were my baby. I made you baby food and fed you, telling you about the theatre, the play, the critics, the other actors. And one day, I heard you talk for the first time. You wanted to know about the market and the street. And I described the market to you, filled with vegetables and fruit. I explained that radishes are red and lettuce bright green, that plums are black, not black-black, but black-purple, like my favourite dress, now faded. I spoke of the streets full of people, of the cafés with their sidewalk tables now that spring was coming, of the traffic, the horns, and the crazy drivers.

Your voice interrupted my description to tell me that walking on the street, hidden among hundreds of anonymous people, was one of your favourite things to do. That it took you away from your loneliness. That you enjoyed the busy feeling, the noise. I remember listening to your voice, soft and low, and wondering what had led you to the life you had chosen to live. How it was that you, with your big, loving eyes, your baby hands, and that beautiful voice, had decided to join the armed resistance to the dictatorship?

The morning bath became a ritual. First you protested—you liked the water lukewarm, you could soap yourself. Little by little, though, you gave in and let me pass the sponge over your punished skin while we listened to Bach, our favourite. We turned it up good and loud so that we could talk normally without the neighbours hearing. And then we had our coffee and the croissants I got used to buying every morning for you, for us.

At night, after work, I found you sitting up in the armchair, waiting for me. I found you open, soft, vulnerable, giving off an inviting warmth. I went right to your core and opened up my own too. In the semi-darkness we drank tea and spoke in whispers about the things we never mentioned in the light of day: your childhood, my childhood; your adolescence, your first love; my adolescence, my first love. And we spoke of our mothers, of our immense love and deep hatred for them, something we would've never admitted to anybody else, not even to ourselves.

On those warm nights you told me about your complete dedication to the revolution, and I told you about mine to the theatre. But more than anything, we discussed our commitment to life, in our own way, and the severity with which we judged ourselves; this almost punishing effort to become more consistent in our thinking, in our actions. Those warm nights I learned that for you, being able to carry a gun had entailed an enormous effort. It had been an achievement, a birth.

Driving through the empty streets, I hurried to arrive quickly at this dark and muffled game of playing at truth, because our coming together was like walking up towards a mirror: it made us see ourselves in the other. Yet it also held the thrill of getting hurt if we walked too quickly or too far.

One day you told me that you were writing something important for me. You'd finish it that day and show it to me when I returned from the theatre. It's something I've thought about a lot since I came back to life, you told me; something very profound that only you can understand.

That night I hurried more than ever. When I opened the door, your faint perfume floated in the house, but the empty space in the armchair hit me hard. I looked for the letter, I looked for your body, but there was nothing. You had walked out without telling me.

I don't know where you went. I don't know if, in this very moment, your small hand grasps a weapon, a weapon I don't condone and against which I fight from my own front. All I know is that I understand you and you understand me. All I know is that your perfume and your image linger, inside my own.

adios piazzolla

I NEVER SAW PIAZZOLLA. Fingers on the bandoneon's keys, moving as if exploring a body made up of little buttons and folds, like mine, made up of buttons that make me think of things, feel things; like this one here, under my arm, which activates laughter; or this other one, on the scruff of my neck, which switches on anguish. Piazzolla, with his fingers on my buttons, rocking me on his knee, like a father or an affectionate grandpa, getting roars of laughter and sighs out of me. Piazzolla, like an expert lover, pushing the buttons of my desires and unfolding me in gaspings and longings.

I never saw Piazzolla, that deep wrinkle between his eyebrows and his little boy's mouth, a sad mouth, perhaps since he said goodbye to his *Nonino*, or perhaps since long before, when his grandparents or his great-grandparents left Italy and went to live in the madness and the pleasures of the *Porteño* summer. What Buenos Aires streets did Piazzolla walk on? What tongues got into his young mouth, into his fingers?

The first time I didn't see Piazzolla was in Buenos Aires. I was one of those members of the Chilean Resistance to the Pinochet regime who spent day after day in a hotel room, going out only to meet somebody who never seemed to show up. All of my buttons were activated: impatience, fear, anger, anguish. And then one day I read in the newspaper that Piazzolla would be playing that Saturday night at the Opera. Anti-dictatorial militants do not carry considerable amounts of money; on the contrary, they stay in cheap hotels and go hungry. I went over my budget at least ten times, ready for any sacrifice, but I had to conclude that even if I decided to stay on the street and not eat for three days, I did not have enough money for a ticket to the concert.

Without thinking twice about it, I decided to risk everything: my safety, my militancy, my dignity. I had to go to this concert. That Saturday night I went to the Opera and watched, filled with jealousy, the arrival of hundreds of *porteños*, loud and well-dressed. I waited until the big rush was over and approached the ticket-man at the door. I explained to him that I was a great admirer of Piazzolla, that I was not from Buenos Aires, that my wallet had been stolen—this, that, and the other. I did this with my best western Argentinean accent (I thought). It did not work. The man stated his *no* like a pighead and would not let me in, not even to listen from the foyer. He made a comment that made me realize that he didn't like Chileans, and then I found out that when I'm overtaken by emotion, the button controlling my Chilean accent gets pushed, and all I can do is go on and on with the diminutives and the Chilean high-pitched sing-song: *No sea malito, pu . . .*

I cried my head off as I walked down the Avenida de Mayo on my way back to the hotel. I didn't care if people were looking or not looking at me, if I was being very conspicuous, if I looked ridiculous, if my makeup was running down my face, nothing. A few blocks down the street I realized what I was doing and panicked. I started to imagine that the man at the theatre had hated me so much that he had phoned the Argentinean police, who in turn had phoned the Chilean secret police, and *they* would be waiting for me at the hotel. I walked around downtown in circles at least five times without knowing what to do. Finally, I called the hotel to ask if there were any messages or if anybody was waiting for me. I listened to the receptionist's voice with my ears and my pores, on the verge of paranoia. I had to conclude that her voice was not quivering and that she sounded attentive and relaxed. The fact that nobody was waiting for me became crystal clear that night of long absences and pain; long, like my country.

The second time I didn't see Piazzolla was in Vancouver. When I knew that he would be playing at the Arts Club, I bought the best tickets in the house. At this point, I had stopped being so poor and my militancy had taken a different form. Preparing painstakingly for the concert, I played my Piazzolla collection everyday, almost secretly, kneading the rhythms, feeling every note elevate me like a kite, taking me back to the streets of Buenos Aires, or making me miss my mother, or my mother tongue. I tried to imagine Piazzolla beyond that only picture of him I had ever seen, his right foot on a chair and the bandoneon resting on his knee, his deep wrinkle, his sad mouth. Lying on the floor, looking at the swirls of smoke from my cigarette rise up and reach the ceiling, I saw him as a child, in short trousers with his big knees sticking out and his hair slicked down with Brancatto Gel. I had decided I had to avenge the man at the Opera once and for all. I was completely determined to enjoy Piazzolla with my whole being.

Two days 'til the concert. A Friday. The phone rings at about four in the afternoon. A woman's voice; impersonal, doing her duty. A car accident. Yes, my name is in his agenda book, to be notified in case of an emergency. Yes, St. Paul's Hospital. No, she is not authorized to tell me about the patient's condition.

The same buttons as in Buenos Aires. Me, alone, waiting for somebody who would never show up, or maybe, somebody who had already come, but . . . would leave forever? What would I do without his Piazzollan fingers playing me, getting sighs and gasps out of my yielding folds?

I stayed with him in the hospital room afternoon, evening, night, dawn, day, noon, afternoon, evening, night, day. . . . I stayed with my *bandoneonista*, the one with his eyes closed and a machine for making "beeps" at the foot of the bed. I did not see Piazzolla. The two best seats in the house were empty at the Arts Club that Sunday night. A few weeks later, Celeste, our Argentinean friend and comrade, told us that it had been grand. *Fenómeno che*, she said. Yes, Piazzolla had played standing up, his right foot on a chair. Yes, he had a deep wrinkle between his eyebrows and the mouth of a sad boy. But he had smiled several times.

The *Clarín* newspaper comes daily to Pizzeria Baires on the corner of Fraser and 49th. That's how we got the news. First, the stroke and the trip from Paris back to Buenos Aires. Then a long period of deterioration, and finally, death. I cried Piazzolla's death the same way I had cried that evening walking down Avenida de Mayo. But perhaps I cried even more for the death of my dream. I never saw Piazzolla. In particular, I didn't see him twice. I still listen to his maestro's fingers. I am not alone. My *bandoneonistas* continue to play my buttons. All of them, the ones that turn on the giggles and the ones that turn on the fears.

i sing, therefore i am

SHE PUSHED WITH EVERYTHING: skin, teeth, fingernails. Soaked in ocean water, she felt a tidal wave open her at her roots and fall loose, head down. Her voice called for her mother, but she was answered by the bloodstained cry of her son, dark and perfect roundness. They placed him on her chest and she felt him, soft, warm, hers. Her son. She laughed lightly, while her hands explored the miniature fingers, the sticky brush of black hair. Then she closed her eyes and slept, relieved.

A sharp pain in her right leg woke her up. The darkness of the forest was full of creaks. The river was calling her with the voices of children playing, dogs hounding. She sang with all her soul: *gracias a la vida que me ha dado tanto.** When her watch told her it was six o'clock, she dragged herself to the river. The water welcomed her with its clear surface and the smoothness of its rocks. She drank to repletion, lying on her belly. Her leg

---

*Thanks to life that has given me so much.

wouldn't let her stand up, and there she decided she could not continue. She was going to die. She was going to die in the Andes, the monumental, the relentless, her friend and enemy. She was going to die without fulfilling her task. Her comrades wouldn't get to know where the weapons were hidden. She cried with the birds, stubbornly reminding her that the lives of others continue when you die. Her son would learn to read without her, fall in love without her. He would go on living without her.

She managed to sit up. With her hand she felt the bulge and swelling on her shin. The pain coursed throughout her body in a torrent. She studied the map, the compass. She wasn't very far. Maybe six more hours of walking. But what would she do if she encountered another rocky mass like the one that had caused the fall? No, she would never get there. She thought of Jack London and Cortázar. The only thing left to do was to die with dignity. She made herself comfortable, facing the sun, and dedicated herself to putting her life in order. She concluded that a computer would have been useful to cut and paste, edit, change spaces, times. She got to the end of her life. Just before the end: the yellow sweater for her son. The yellow sweater that now rested, with no sleeves, in the knitting basket, by the armchair. Who was going to finish the sleeves for her son's yellow sweater?

She took off her parka, her pullover, and her undershirt. With the undershirt she made long bandages and tied up her leg. Then she put the pullover and the parka back on. Her hand reached out for a stick that was floating in the river. She stood and began to walk, using the stick for a cane. She had to live so that she could finish the sleeves for her son's sweater.

She walked in the river, the water up to her waist, her eyes swimming in salty water, the only warm thing in that geography. She felt the sky go dark with clouds over her head, the rain run down her neck, into her ears. She went on walking. Thunder, lightning began. She went on walking. She saw gigantic trees, prehistoric ferns. She went on walking. Now she could feel the meeting point on the map, in the forest, by the river. She went on walking, dreaming of hugs—Rulo's, Flaca's, Negros's hugs, her comrades' hugs.

She was greeted by a slap on the face from a man in uniform.

She felt herself fall in an abyss of ice. She was awakened by an acute pain between her legs, a stab that turned to throbs going up her back. She opened her eyes. The spotlights of the torture chamber blinded her. She called out for her mother. The nasal voice of a man answered: your mommy is not here, Lorena. I am here, your sugar daddy. Sing, Lorena, sing. Where are the weapons? She sang with all her soul: *Gracias a la vida que me ha dado tanto*. You sing beautifully, the voice said; but that's not the song we want to hear. The electric shock burned her left breast and spread with roars of mocking laughter up her neck.

She dreamed that her mother was taking her by the hand through the clouds towards an orange tree full of fruit. Her son was sitting on a branch, peeling an orange. She took him in her arms and as she walked behind her mother, he put sections of the orange in her mouth, one by one. Her son had the yellow sweater on, with no sleeves.

She opened her eyes and from the ceiling she saw a naked woman, sitting astride a uniformed man's legs; the man's fly was open. His hands were kneading the woman's butt and his mouth was biting her nipples. The woman looked familiar, but she was missing her right leg. The woman, her dark hair down to her shoulders, was moaning, her arms at her sides, inert. She pulled her away and took her in her arms. The woman was cold. She rocked her and cuddled her to warm her up. She kissed her sweetly on the nose, the cheeks. They fell asleep entwined.

She was awakened by the blaring radio and the nasal voice of the man with the open fly: this *puta* doesn't sing, my lieutenant. Maybe this whore doesn't know, my lieutenant. We don't know what else to do to her, my lieutenant. I think she doesn't know.

She doesn't know. She doesn't know how to walk with crutches. Her right leg isn't there anymore, but it still hurts. She's alive. *I hurt, therefore I am.* Her mother, her son, and the cultural attaché to the embassy are waiting for her. A car with diplomatic plates followed by a military jeep take them to the airport. Her country, long and narrow, stays down there, framed by the salty water of the Pacific Ocean and the mute stature of the Andes. The yellow sweater, with no sleeves, is in her handbag. Her son will need the sleeves before winter arrives in Canada. It's very cold there. She closes her eyes and knits and knits, while she feels her son asleep on her chest, and her mother's hand patting her dark hair, down to her shoulders.

in the company of words

HEY PILAR VALLEJO, REMEMBER WHEN we used to run down Ferrari Street and the boats looked so small down there in the bay and we were so goofy, pretending to be nuts, and then we hung around on the corner with our hands in our pockets and whistled *Madame Butterfly* arias after my brother took us to the Victoria to see the movie with Mario Lanza?

And remember School Number 20 on top of Bellavista Hill, those starched, white girls, ruffles and ribbons, shiny shoes and circles of Nugget shoe polish on our ankle socks, girls reciting *Piececitos de Niño*, times tables, Arturo Prat's last words: *all aboard, boys*; and you raising your hand, saying, Miss Graciela, I think he was pushed, and Miss Graciela putting you in the corner for being a smartass and me making faces at you, throwing paper airplanes with messages inside?

And remember Mondays, when we were all spotless, even you and me, singing the national anthem at the top of our lungs in the playground of the Girls' School Number 20, listening to the boys across the street, the ones from the *Men's* School Number 19, singing the national anthem at the top of *their* lungs but a little ahead or behind us? It was pandemonium, but finally we all finished together with Sanfuentes Street between us, *o el asilo contra la opresión*, oh shelter from oppression, oh shelter from oppression, oh shelter from oppression, da-da-da-da-da-da-da-da-da-da-da-dah, PA-PA-PUM.

If only they'd seen us, Pilar Vallejo, riding the scooter my Aunt Luca gave me, flying downhill, you in front and me in the back, stuck to you like a barnacle, watching the Vargas' house come upon us from under your arm and holding a high C so strong and clear, even Madame Butterfly would have been impressed. And you swerving in the last fraction of a second, but we kept on flying, nothing to stop us now but the Blessed Virgin, oh my God, why didn't I listen to my mother, eyes closed and everything red, everything red, and you saying, did you see that, silly goose, we won and nothing happened. . . . Yeah, nothing happened, except my broken arm, with no elbow or wrist, dangling from somewhere in between like the head of the kitchen mop, and that imbecile Gloria Bobadilla singing, *I'm telling your mo-om, I'm telling your mo-om.*

Oh Pilar Vallejo, so many years have passed since that day I asked you about your mother, and you, blushing like a tomato, told me she was dead and that was that, and I wanted to know how did she die, what did she die of, and you said she was dead and that was that and then, insatiably curious and already quite the extortionist, I said if you didn't tell me, I wouldn't play with you anymore or lend you my dolls, or the scooter, or anything else. But right away I regretted it and I hugged you because now you were crying and whispering, *From the abortion, from the abortion,* and I didn't understand a thing, but I comforted you anyway and made out as if I understood, and cried with you knowing I couldn't ask my mother or anyone because *from the abortion* reeked of secrecy and evil, and if Mama knew, it'd be goodbye to the invitations to Pilar Vallejo for tea and cookies, goodbye to going to the movies with Pilar Vallejo, goodbye to Pilar Vallejo, amen.

So many things have happened since then and sometimes, like now, stuck on the empty streets of this Vancouver suburb, stuck in this autoland, stuck missing Ferrari Street, with the neighbourhood kids playing soccer, hopscotch, and jump rope, stuck missing the Ideal Bakery and their pork buns at four in the afternoon, stuck in this interminable Vancouver lushness, I think about you, Pilar Vallejo, and I wonder what's become of your life, if you went to high school, if you got married or lived in sin, if you had kids, if you ever left the hills of Valparaíso to roam like me.

I'm okay—more or less. Just think, Pilar Vallejo, I'm under another sky and another sun, far from Valparaíso. My parents wait for the mailman in their house in Quilpué and look for my brother, who disappeared the eleventh of September, 1973. In Canada, I'm learning to speak again and trying somehow to make sense out of life here. I'm a janitor in a skyscraper in downtown Vancouver. From the thirty-second floor, I can see the boats in the bay—tiny, like the ones we used to see from Bellavista Hill, almost thirty years ago.

Who knows, one of these years when I come back, maybe we'll run into each other, strolling through Plaza Victoria. We could go see what Ferrari Street looks like now, and afterwards I'd buy you an ice cream at Bogarín's.

By the way, now I know the meaning of the word abortion.

saudades

GRANDMA FLORA SLOWLY LOOKS OVER the yellowed photograph, her mouth chewing away on who-knows-what memories. Only her hands seem to be in any hurry; from under the table comes the steady click-click of the knitting needles. Nobody seems to be bothered by the silence. Only me, the intruder from a world where every pause must be filled with words.

The mouth continues chewing, the eyes moving back and forth across the photo. A half-finished child's toque appears from under the table and is laid to rest on top of a book. Grandma Flora's left hand takes hold of the photograph and her right forefinger, time-worn and calloused, goes over the brick building, the small windows, and the group of dark children dressed in suits and boots, standing on the entrance steps. Her mouth stops chewing and she says:

The children look sad. They all look sad. You can see the suffering. They're far from their families. They can't speak their language. The school is like a prison.

My friend Adriana, the literacy teacher, writes what Grandma

Flora says on the blackboard, in big, round letters. Adriana's hand is an extension of Grandma Flora's mouth. I, the visitor, just watch. Adriana reads aloud what she has written, pointing at each word, each syllable. Grandma Flora copies it all down in her notebook. When she has finished, her ancient voice merges with Adriana's distant accent as the two read together, their fingers moving across the paper, prying, as if the profound truth of so many broken lives were buried within those letters, words, spaces.

At the end of the class, Adriana and I walk back in silence to her place, followed by the dogs from the reserve. Children play hockey on the dirt streets, smoke rises from the chimneys and blends with the dampness of the forest. The water keeps rushing onward, just like then, just like always. We pause to watch how the river flows into the sea. The impoverished houses are behind us now, as the eternity of the ocean fills our eyes, our ears, our noses, our pores.

Grandma Flora didn't go to the residential school that the white man's government carefully designed to assimilate the Indians. Her brother Charlie did. Their land had already been taken away. They were living on reserves. Alcoholism had taken root and begun to spread like fire. Government agents had taken the children off to the school in Tofino. Only the youngest ones were left. And Flora and Charlie.

Flora and Charlie imagining that far-off place full of dark-skinned children singing to the Queen, dressed in uniforms, learning the language of the white man, kneeling down to pray to an almighty god. Flora and Charlie fishing in this river, barefoot, laughing, laughing, speaking in sounds that taste of earth, hopping back and forth over those stones. Flora and

Charlie hiding in the woods on their mother's orders when word came that the agent was on his way. Flora and Charlie hiding up in that tree, whistling like birds, making fun of that thing their mother called "the government," the thing that wanted to take away everything, including the children, and would never give them back.

That evening Adriana cooks a Canadian version of her far-away Brazilian *feiojada* while we listen to Maria Betania:

Sonho meu, sonho meu
Vai buscar quem mora longe, sonho meu
Vai mostrar esta saudade, sonho meu
A madrugada fria so metraz maelancolia, sonho meu

Dream of mine, dream of mine, go off and find someone who lives far away. Go off and show him this *saudade*, this longing. The cold dawn only brings me sadness, dream of mine. From the mouth of the wind comes the song of this island on the edge of the map. The trees, the ancient peoples, the rain. The *samba* is so far away, dream of mine. The night rumbles with the echo of Grandma Flora's voice:

You can see the suffering
You can see the suffering

After dinner Adriana tells me the end of the story behind the yellowed photograph, behind Grandma Flora's mouth and hands: Charlie got tired of hiding from the government agent and went off to the residential school with his hair slicked down and a big smile on his face. He was eleven years old then. He never came back. Two years later, the government sent a letter saying that he had run away. His mother didn't cry. Flora went out to throw stones into the river. They didn't look for him. Five years later, someone told them they had seen him in Vancouver. Flora went to look for him, to bring him back. Neither of them returned. They got lost in the bars of Hastings Street. Flora came back when she was thirty. When she was forty, with six children living and three dead, she said: *I am an alcoholic.* She still says it, but she hasn't had a drink in twenty-eight years.

I am not going back to Adriana's class. I will not see Grandma Flora again. My own life calls me back to Vancouver. The visit has come to an end. Adriana walks me to the bus. In the morning fog we linger in one of those hugs that enclose much shared hope. Sometimes we pursue our dreams a long way away from where we were born. My friend's silhouette fades off in the distance; her left fist is raised high. I respond, raising mine. I am taking Grandma Flora's face etched between my eyebrows.

Back in the city, I spend months looking for Charlie. I ask in all the bars, the hotels, the community centres, the liquor stores. There can't be very many who survived into old age like him. I don't know why I'm looking for him. What am I going to say to him when I find him? That I met his sister Flora on a visit to Port Hardy? That my Brazilian friend is teaching her how to read? That Flora is fine, that she hasn't had a drink for twenty-eight years? That I am interested in the situation of First Nations people? That I am from Latin America and that our First Nations have also suffered very much? Perhaps I have turned into a fucking liberal after all! I don't find him. Nobody knows him. Charlie doesn't exist.

A few months later Adriana is on the phone, crying. Charlie died in the Vancouver General Hospital. He was there for a week. Nobody notified the family. They didn't have to get rid of the body until now.

More news: today Grandma Flora wrote a story by herself, by her own hand, for the first time.

hand-made times

I'VE COME TO THE END OF THE PATH. While you're playing at home, daughter of mine, I'm here at the end of the path. The local radio stations have already gone off the air. Marches have replaced the last-minute warnings and the military commands are polluting our ears, our minds, and our hands with their sinister vomit. While you play at home, daughter of mine, I'm here at the end of the path. We're all here; friends and *compañeros* have all come to the university this crisp spring day. We've all come and we're waiting. From eight to ten I have to teach the translation class; I've got it prepared—we'll do some children's stories, like "Peter Rabbit." Only today, I'm not waiting for my students.

When I was a kid, we weren't allowed to play with toy guns. My brothers played ball; I played with dolls. Sometimes we played with our friends' water pistols. We would run down the street after the other kids, shooting the water pistols at them; afterwards, we would hide in the alley. When we came home all soaked, our mother would send us to bed.

Roberto came, he says that we have to wait, that they'll be here soon.

When we went to the fair—remember when we took you to

Bustamante Park in Santiago?—I wasn't able to hit the ducks with that rifle. I shot at everything except the ducks. We had more fun on the Ferris wheel and the merry-go-round. You wanted to try the rifle but I wouldn't let you.

Five people have gone to watch the bridge, to wait there, so that they can give us the warning call.

When the discussions about a possible coup began, I just didn't want to think about it. I never believed those who insisted that the day would come when we would have to defend ourselves. I didn't want to believe them. What happened to our peaceful road to socialism? Allende was elected by popular vote. The Chilean military are supposed to be professionals and their job is to defend the elected government, not to overthrow it. I thought that these things only happened in the so-called "banana republics," not in Chile.

We've lined up and are jogging now. It's been so long since I've jogged. I think the last time was in high school, in phys-ed class. It's amazing how I've let myself go. I can't run half a block without getting out of breath. You're playing at home, daughter of mine.

They say they're Soviet, that they'll be here soon. They say we should've been prepared, that it's a shame, that we had enough warning. They say that the right-wing capitalists are all prepared. They have been bringing them over the border, from Argentina: American, brand-name Gloria. I wonder now if that's what was in the boxes that the neighbours were unloading from a pick-up truck a couple of weeks ago. I woke up at three a.m. to the sound of muffled voices on the street; peeked out the window and saw Dr. Vergara and two other men carrying long boxes into the house.

After the 1960 earthquake, my dad was given two pistols to guard the school where he was the principal. Our house was right next door. He kept the pistols locked up in the dining-room cabinet and never allowed us to hold them. One night, my mom heard a noise and went out to the garden alone with one of the pistols. The blasts woke us up. My mother had killed a cat, thinking it was thieves.

Mariana is explaining how to hold them. She says you just have to hold them with confidence. She says they are light and easy to handle. Now we have to practice throwing ourselves to the ground. I wonder what it will be like holding a real one in my hands. I only know how to hold children and books. I have small, soft hands. You like it when I scratch your head with these hands, or tickle your nose or hold you and cuddle you when you're sleepy. We're all face down on the grass now, pretending we have one in our hands. I wonder if I'll be able to pull the trigger.

Strange noises can be heard on the other side of the river. Your bald doll, the one that was mine and is now yours, must be dressed by now; maybe you are changing her clothes, or are you singing to her?

The ones that were waiting on the bridge are running towards us. They say that they're coming now, that they're crossing the bridge. It's hard to hear, the noise is terrible, the earth shakes. We have to be ready. We get into lines to receive them. In the sky, the army helicopters look like dragonflies with huge eyes, watching us. The city groans on the other side of the river.

Now we can see the American tanks in the street with the poplars. The tanks have blocked all the accesses. They have come to the end of the path. Green insects drag along the asphalt, their hands holding American submachine guns. We have to run to the river. With empty hands, we have to run to the river. Maybe we'll manage to find a boat, maybe they won't shoot, maybe they'll concede us the right to life.

With empty hands I run downhill, reach the bank and jump onto the moving boat. Bullets whiz by my ears and hit the water. I duck down, trying to find cover, like in the television cop movies that we sometimes watch together. But this is not a movie and I am not a criminal.

Roberto's lying at my feet, on the bottom of the boat, his white shirt soaked in blood. I hear Mariana's moans behind me. A bullet has perforated her thigh. I look at the dozen or so familiar faces that surround me, in search of comfort, but I find only sadness and fear. The sound of my own sobbing brings me back to my body as I feel the warmth and weight of Carlos' arm resting on my shoulders.

I think about the years to come, about the promises that I made you, daughter of mine, the better life we wanted for you and all Chilean children. And I make you one final promise: tomorrow, when we're ready again to retrieve life and the future, our hands will not be empty.

trespass

IT'S TRUE, *COMADRE*, NO MONEY FOR CARPETS HERE—at most, the mattress on the floor, kerosene for the hot plate and cigarettes. Can't get along without those. It's a different life altogether, no question about that. But the difference doesn't only lie in the lack of material comfort. No—it also lies in the lack of comfort for the mind and the stomach. But I can't complain, *comadre*, I don't have to be concerned with diets anymore. This lifestyle does wonders for my figure!

In Vancouver we never imagined what life underground would really be like. It's a full-time job, and I don't mean eight hours a day, but twenty-four. The tasks can be extremely boring or, once in a while, very dangerous. Life underground is no bowl of cherries, *comadre*, that's for sure. And on top of everything else, you can't even talk about your past or present life with *anybody*.

But I can speak to you, *comadre*, anytime I want and about whatever I want. All I have to do is plug you into my head and there we go. I can tell you things, remember things. . . . Somehow I know you can hear me up north. I send you these telepathic messages and then I feel better, relieved, lighter, happier.

I always remember that you went on and on about your fears about our personal safety, insisting that I had to take care of myself and the girls. And you were right, *comadre*. Yes, I have to take good care of myself, I can't let the military get me. I feel terrified thinking that they may do something to the girls. Even though they are safe living with my mom and dad, I still worry. The most important thing is to follow all the security measures to the letter. Next week I will have to move again, find a room in a different *barrio*. That's one of the basic principles in this kind of work: never stay anywhere for more than a month, and never give your address to anybody. But it's tiring having to look for a new *pensión* every month, having to make sure I don't run into people I know, carrying all my stuff to new places—not that I have a lot, but still.

One of the hardest things to get used to has been my new name. Remember when we used to joke about having a new name and inventing a whole new life for ourselves, a life just like the one we would've liked to have, with all the fantasies we wanted? Well, that's not the way it works, *comadre*. Besides, I've discovered that, in spite of everything, my own life has not been so bad. I actually like it a lot and feel weird about having to learn the story of a borrowed life. The only thing I don't like and would like to change is the separation from Sergio. I wish he hadn't fallen in love with that *gringa* and left me. But, *c'est la vie*, you can't force anybody to stay in love with you, right?

Just think, *comadre*, I'm supposed to be a student of history at the Catholic University. I'm from Frutillar and that's why I live in a *pensión* in Santiago. I'm young and single, and given that I'm a real nerd, I don't have a boyfriend or even girlfriends.

That's why nobody visits me. So, I've had to stop wearing my contacts and go back to the good old awful glasses that make my eyes look like dots. Can you imagine? I look horrible. Now I have my hair long and straight—had to say goodbye to my perms and makeup, and carry a schoolbag full of boring history books. In this kind of life, those are the kinds of things you have to do in order to stay safe.

But I do enjoy becoming someone completely different once in a while, for short periods of time, when I need to do a very specific task. Like the other day, when I had to go to the Ministry of the Interior to find out about V.I.P. passports (yes, there are special passports for "important" people in Chile now). I went with a *compañero* named Raúl. We were supposed to be a married couple from San Fernando, owners of vineyards and wineries, wanting to take a trip to Asia to promote our products. I wore a rose-coloured skirt-and-blazer suit with a black silk shirt, and black leather pumps and purse. I also wore stockings, a short brown wig with a bobcut, and golden jewelry. My fingernails were polished in rosy pink (almost the same colour as my suit) and I had discreet but visible make-up on. The wig was sort of a pain in the ass—or on the head, rather—because it was itchy. Otherwise, everything went well and for a while I even felt sort of attractive.

What I like the most about these short, daring little tasks is the satisfaction of knowing that we have trespassed the limits, passed the boundaries of the dictatorship's territory; that even though the military is so powerful, it is also very vulnerable; that we can tap on its vulnerability to get to know it better, in order that we can sweep it out. It's a great feeling. When I think about this I cannot help remembering Lautaro, the way Neruda describes him in *Canto General*, or the way my mother used to tell

me his life story when I was a kid. Lautaro, the Mapuche
hereditary chief who was trained from birth to lead his people
in the war of resistance against the Spanish *conquistadores*. His
elders used a combination of love and discipline until, as a
teenager, he was ready to infiltrate Pedro de Valdivia's house and
become his personal servant. For years, he lived with the *conquistador*, attending to all his needs and learning everything he
could about him and his ways. He even helped him in many of
the battles against the Mapuche. But when he was ready, he went
back to his people and led them in the triumphant war that ended
with Valdivia's death and the decimation of the Spanish army.

> *Llegó Lautaro en traje de relámpago.*
> . . .
> *De tumbo en tumbo la capitanía*
> *iba retrocediendo desangrada.*
>
> *Ya se tocaba el pecho de Lautaro,*
> *Valdivia vio venir la luz, la aurora,*
> *tal vez la vida, el mar.*
> > *Era Lautaro.*

> *Lautaro arrived draped in lightning.*
> . . .
> *Stumbling and bleeding*
> *the conquistadores retreated*
>
> *One could touch Lautaro's heart now,*
> *Valdivia saw the coming of light, dawn,*
> *maybe life, ocean water.*
> > *It was Lautaro.*

Remember, *comadre*, when we read Neruda's poem about Lautaro in one of our public presentations and people began to cry, taken up by emotion? It was such an intense experience!

But enough of that for now and back to this feeling-ugly-most-of-the-time business. Other than making me a little depressed once in a while, it doesn't have great implications because I have no hope of having a relationship or even a fling. That's part of life underground. So, I'm screwed. Or rather, I'm not. . . .

Let me tell you something, *comadre*. The other day I spent a couple of hours with a *compañero* I had never met before. I loved the way he carried himself and I think he liked me too, in spite of my nerdy look. There was lots of electricity going on between us. We talked about everything we needed to talk about regarding work and then it became obvious that neither one of us wanted to leave. So, since I couldn't really tell him anything about my life, I told him about a dream I had the other night, a dream about telephones.

I was in this place where there were dozens of phones all over the place—on the walls, the tables, the floor, everywhere. I went from one telephone to the next saying hello, hello, but all the phones were either dead, didn't have a tone, or had their cables cut. I woke up sweating like a pig and crying in the middle of the night. Luis (that's his name) told me that it was natural for us to have those kinds of dreams because in fact we are sort of incommunicado, can't really talk about anything with anybody and that makes life hard, very hard. And while he was saying this I was looking at him like a stupid idiot, wishing he would touch me, hold my hand, put his arm around my shoulders, take my face in both his hands. . . . I felt like crying, looking at him at the other side of the table of the café where we met. But I was able to control myself and felt very proud because not one tear came out of my eyes. I just smiled at him and nodded, as if nothing was happening. But when I got to my room I cried my eyes out.

I also fantasized about Luis....

Luis your nakedness haunts me like a yielding dark simple ample open clean hand you curl curve stretch in between my fingers on the tip of my tongue I put you in my mouth piece by piece become a miniature in your arms get tangled in the hair on your chest offer you my dampness my breasts cradle you follow your skin of a rabbit find refuge in your eyes tremble become an ocean invite you in you submerge arrive Luis Lucho compañero I reveal myself to you open you up contemplate caress lick suck kiss get inside you put you inside me we go crazy erupt live here and now in with from our bodies turn the night into an endless explosion celebrate our own revolution love until we're torn to shreds pant sweat laugh we love each other compañero Luis....

Remember, *comadre*, when we read the letters that Alexandra Kollontai sent to Clara Zetkin back in the twenties? There was one in which she talked about what it meant for her to be a revolutionary woman and about the loneliness she experienced. And she also talked about her envy of her male comrades, because she knew that they had women waiting for them, keeping a home for them, cooking, bringing up the children; and when they returned from a long journey into the underground or from a long day of work, they always had a place to go to, a hot dish on the table, a pair of arms to welcome and cradle them, to give them strength.

The other night, after meeting Luis, I thought a lot about Kollontai and cried for her and all the women who have decided to pursue this kind of life in spite of the difficulties. But just thinking that Kollontai was the only woman who became a member of the central committee of the Bolshevik party and a minister in Lenin's government also gave me strength. When I think about that, sparks run up and down my spine.

Comadre, don't worry about the girls. They are doing very well living with my mom and dad. I see them once a week for a few minutes, everytime in a different place. We kiss and hug, and then I have to go. It's difficult, but it's beautiful too. My poor ma brings me a package with homemade bread and cookies, a block of *chanco* cheese, and beef jerky and apples that my godmother sends from her farm. The old man whispers anti-dictatorial speeches in my ear and tells me that he's very proud of me, that not even his sons turned out to be such good revolutionaries. I don't know what I would do without my mom and dad.

And here I am, *comadre*, a Sunday in August, lying on my bed after having visited with my old folks and my daughters, talking to you and listening to the Susana Rinaldi tape that you used to like so much. We listened to it together, for the last time, that summer afternoon in Vancouver, almost a year ago, lying on the carpet in your living room, silently, knowing that never again, never again. . . .

Malena canta el tango como ninguna
y en cada verso pone su corazón

Malena sings the tango like no one else
and commits her heart to every verse

"My heart is committed, but I'm afraid. I can't go," you said. In silence, we left the house and walked to the beach. Jericho Park bustled with people and Vancouver spread out like a vision on the other side of the bay.... *Comadre*, I never thought I would miss Vancouver when I came back to Chile. But sometimes, particularly when fear wants to take over my body and my mind, I think of Vancouver and feel a lot better. Then, I would give anything to be there again, even if it were for just a few minutes, sitting on a log on the beach, looking at the ocean, the sailboats, the city on the other side of the water with its cement and crystal monuments stretching up to the sky, their hundreds of eyes lighting up in the twilight while the sun burns the sky, Stanley Park sticking its green tongue into the inlet, the mountains, a backdrop with their woods and snow-capped peaks....

Vancouver I never loved you while I lived in you and now I want you miss you I allow myself to walk on Commercial Drive buy a dozen rossettas at Renato's bakery have a glass of wine at the Caffé Central with Roger and Sandra enjoy a plate of gnocchi de la nona at Nick's while we change the world with words I take the Granville bus towards Chinatown go into every shop look at the miniatures fans statuettes notebooks with silk-lined covers walk into the alley behind Pender knock on the Green Door ask for a won-ton soup with barbecued duck lick my lips walk to Hastings take the McDonald bus get off in Kitsilano I allow myself to walk on Fourth Avenue with its boutiques cafés bookstores sit down at El Cerrito drink a cappuccino go into the Kitchen Corner look at the soup bowls plates teapots ladles spoons knives cups placemats napkins strainers funnels lemon squeezers bread baskets butter dishes big small medium salad bowls made of clay china green white grey brown come out with a blue glass juice jug walk happily around smile cross the street take the UBC bus to my daughters' school where they're waiting for me skipping-girl's walk sing get home have their afternoon milk with the cookies I made last night all the kids in the neighbourhood love the cookies that Camila and Alejandra's mom makes there they come Jessica Komiko Teddy Lucas Andrea Gloria Chris Jesse Della I allow myself to go back to my Vancouver home sit at the kitchen table lie on my own bed read a story to my daughters. . . .

That afternoon you had fifty dollars to make a "contribution to the cause," and you went on and on about the fifty dollars and the contribution, insisting that I needed a good-looking outfit, that I needed to think about my cover. . . .

Two hours in the boutiques on Fourth Avenue and Broadway, trying clothes on, looking at myself in the mirror, turning this way, that way, yes, I like it, but we have to let it out here and take the hem up, no . . . maybe not that one . . . this one, if we take it in at the top and let it out on the hips . . . too bad it's sewn right to the edge . . . this one will be okay if we shorten the straps . . . but developed dresses don't fit under-developed women; the image in the mirror, ridiculous . . . for the six-foot types . . . and the hips . . . me, with my hippopotamus rump. . . .

Frustrated, we went back to your house, *comadre*, picked up the guitar and the *charango* and started to sing. We were so good together, from the protest songs to the *sambas* and *bossanovas*, not to mention the *boleros*, plus all those songs in English we learned with the help of our friend Pat. . . .

There once was a union maid she never was afraid of the goons and the ginks and the company finks and the deputy sheriffs that made the raid . . . and one and two and one and two with the charanguito . . . who would've ever imagined dear armadillo that one day you would wake up as a charango singing union songs in English up in Canada . . . you who were born in the

87

Altiplano to sing with the wind and the llamas ... ay I would give anything to have a charango or a guitar to accompany me in a tango or a bolero ... the door closed behind you and you never came back la la la li liri lirí taririririri lará. ...

Remember that time, *comadre*, when we crossed the Rockies in a blizzard in the middle of the night? Scott had lent us his Volkswagen van to travel with our singing group to Calgary and Edmonton and then on a tour of B.C. on our way back. But we almost stayed in the Rockies, buried in snow with the van and everything else! And the only thing that stupid René could think of saying was that the Andes were a lot taller and that blizzards there were *real* blizzards. ... But at least Pablo and Carlos sang like crazy the whole way, trying to keep our spirits up, even though it was not an easy task.

I have never felt as cold as I felt that night, *comadre*. I remember driving the van without being able to see anything and then realizing that the heater wasn't working. ... We tried pulling and turning every knob but nothing worked and I started feeling like a statue, stiff like an iceberg. Everything started to hurt—my temples, knees, shoulders—with an acute pain that felt like needles. ... But miraculously we made it to Calgary. Our *compañeros* and *compañeras* were dead worried, waiting for us with hot tea and *sopaipillas*. ...

Chileans in Calgary and Edmonton poor and rich some like any other exiled Chileans like us with commitment and memories others gone crazy with the oil boom hard but good-paying jobs three cars in the garage dining-room sets living-room sets bedroom sets crystalware silverware displayed in curios satellite dishes on the roof Chilean television Mexican Brazilian Colom-

bian soaps señoras knitting and bawling their eyes out señores
watching the Colo Colo soccer game on a Saturday afternoon
too bad compañero that we have to boycott Chilean wine but
French wine is not bad of course not man it's considered to be
the best in the world but for me Concha y Toro is the best no way
around it let's see what are we going to wear for tonight's peña
look at how good Señora María looks in her long red-sequinned
dress and her patent leather shoes that make her feet look like
empanadas spilling out and over her fine elegant expensive
Italian footwear that she bought at Eaton's and don Manuel in
his gold lamé jacket dancing like a Valentino one two three one
two three oh how far my country is but how close or maybe it is
because there is a land where all blood is mixed la la la one two
three from Alberta to the Kootenays where Canadian union
members feminists anti-Vietnam war activists are waiting for us
we go through Nelson Cranbrook Kimberley Kaslo Castlegar
and then Penticton Kelowna Winfield Peachland Summerland
sweet green Okanagan valley lakes and fields covered with
grapes apples I allow myself to travel again camp by the Shuswap
eat a bowl of strawberries lie face up absorb the sun listen to the
train greeting me on its way to Toronto Montreal where it will
arrive in five days I allow myself to feel the nostalgia I never felt
before. . . .

Comadre, I still remember the names of all those towns we
went to. In some places the public didn't even know where Chile
was, let alone what had happened there. . . . So we talked and
sang and at the end everybody was on their feet with their left
fists up in the air, singing *Trabajadores al Poder*, but there was
no way they could say *Trabajadores* and everybody shouted
Trajabadores al Poder and even *we* ended up shouting *Tra-*

jaba*dores al Poder* and then in the bathroom we laughed so hard, we peed in our pants.

We even had to learn how to pray so that we could get the Christians to support us. The first time we went to talk to a congregation in New Westminster, on a grey and rainy Sunday morning, the priest all of a sudden asked us to say the "Our Father" in Spanish. And the two of us stood up there looking at him with our mouths open, because neither one knew the "Our Father" in Spanish and then I started making everything up, please don't forget about us, we promise to behave and forgive our trespasses because they are very small and for a good cause, but above all don't forget our children and give us some bread for them, please, our hands crossed over our chests, looking at the floor, amen.

Remember that last afternoon of my life as an exile in Vancouver? We talked about so many things, *comadre*. About your childhood as the daughter of rich landowners in the Rancagua region, mine as the child of a miner and a seamstress. About how, coming from such different backgrounds, we ended up sharing the same ideals, and how destiny brought us together ten thousand kilometres from where we were born. And now we were going in different directions, me to join the underground resistance in Chile, you to continue your life as an exile in Canada.

Malena tiene pena de bandoneón

Malena feels the sorrow of a bandoneon

You were right to be afraid, *comadre*. But fear is not insurmountable, and now, more than ever there is hope. There are no words to describe to you how happy I would be to hear that you have decided to come back and that maybe one day we will meet and even do some tasks together.

But that summer afternoon in Vancouver, we knew that it would be a long time before we met again. And today, as I smoke my Hiltons and shiver in the Santiago winter cold, I miss you, *comadre*: I touch you, look at you, talk to you, hug you, just like I did so many times up there, in Canada.

Tu canción tiene el eco del último encuentro
tu canción se hace amarga en la sal del recuerdo

Your song has the echo of our last encounter
your song becomes bitter in the salt of remembrance

I will never forget our "trespasses," *comadre*, particularly those of our last afternoon together.

The ocean was cold. No matter how hot it gets up north, the water is always cold. The moon started to come out and we had to get dressed because if the cops caught us stark naked on the beach. . . .

"I can't see you off, eh?"

"No, *comadre*."

"Can you write to me?"

"No, *comadre*."

"Be careful, *comadre*."

"Yes, *comadre*."

"Here's the fifty dollars. They'll come in handy."

"Thanks, *comadre*."

"I'll keep doing what I can up here until I'm brave enough to go back, *comadre*."

"Okay, *comadre*."

Life is no tango, but shit, it sure seems like it sometimes. The last thing I saw of you, *comadre*, was your back, and the way it carried the weight of your pain.

I'm waiting. I'm waiting for you.

3-D

ELEVEN-FORTY-SIX SALSBURY DRIVE, VANCOUVER, CANADA. Second floor, first door on the left. A medium-sized bedroom with a large window facing north. An expanse of clear blue sky broken up by snow-capped mountain peaks. Next to the double-locked door, a small dresser, painted white.

A tape is playing on a portable cassette deck; on the empty case, Mercedes Sosa stands holding a microphone in her left hand, her body wrapped in a black poncho. Several other cassettes are carefully lined up against the wall: Quilapayún, Violeta Parra, Inti Illimani, Charo Cofré, Tiempo Nuevo, Angel Parra, Víctor Jara, Isabel Parra.

A half-opened drawer is filled with neatly arranged underwear: white cotton bikini panties, lace-trimmed bras, multi-coloured socks, and a few pairs of pantyhose rolled up into balls and tucked in behind the rest.

On the other side of the dresser, a folding door opens into a cupboard where a few clothes are hung: two summer dresses, one long-sleeved white shirt, a grey wool skirt, a pair of black dress pants, and a blue coat, crumpled up on the floor on top of a pair of white running shoes.

A narrow bed is pushed up against the wall on the right. It is covered with a wool blanket with black and red Mapuche designs. A flannel nightgown with a pattern of baby blue flowers lies at the foot of the bed; a pair of pink plush slippers peeks out from underneath.

On the wall above the bed, an assortment of photographs and drawings are tacked up with push pins: a couple in their fifties pose solemnly, arm in arm; a young man of about twenty contemplates the world with half-closed eyes and perfect white teeth; a group of girls laugh and pull faces in a town square. Pencil drawings of flowers, mountains, faces, houses, trees, all signed "Gloria," fill the rest of the bare spaces.

On the wall to the left, there is a poster of Víctor Jara, smiling. In the foreground, his hands hold a guitar with words imprinted on it:

Levántate y mírate las manos
para crecer, estréchala a tu hermano
Juntos iremos, unidos por la sangre
Ahora y en la hora de nuestra muerte
Amén

Rise up and look at your hands
Take your brothers and sisters' hands
Together we'll go forth, united by blood
Now and at the time of our death
Amen

Beneath the poster, a few books, notepads and papers are piled on a small desk. A sketchpad is opened to the unfinished drawing of a man's face. A ceramic cup holds a few pens and pencils. The *Velásquez Spanish-English Dictionary* and a book entitled *English for New Canadians* occupy the centre of the desk. Cortázar's *Todos los Fuegos el Fuego* lies open, face down. On top of it is an open notebook; a page has been ripped out. A pencil has fallen to the floor, along with the missing page.

Between the desk and the bed lies the body of a young woman. Her hair is long, silky, black; her skin is pale, her eyes are green, barely open. Her thin lips are twisted into a faint grimace. She is wearing jeans, a sky-blue hand-knitted sweater, and black leather boots. Her hands are like a child's, from the bitten nails down to the tiny wrists, now opened up like gaping mouths spewing forth a red liquid that is soaking through the sky-blue sweater, the jeans, the white cotton underwear, the lace-trimmed bra and the beige carpet where a razor blade lies next to the fallen pencil and the page torn from the notebook, on which a note has been scrawled:

February 22, 1975
Today I saw him walking down Commercial Drive. He saw me too. He recognized me. He stood there, watching me, a smirk on his face. I couldn't even scream. I never thought he would come all the way to Canada. What is he doing here? It was real, he was there. He recognized me. He'll find out where I live. I can't go on like this. My torturer is here, in Vancouver.

accented living

Facing the ocean, I'm one
Another one when I turn
My head swarms with farewells
Longings burn in my chest
—GABRIELA MISTRAL

BEFORE I LEFT, WILMA HAD GIVEN ME little parcels for the whole family. "This one is for Uncle Werner and this one for Aunt Veronika's kids," she instructed, "and if you can, go to Beccar to Uncle Otto's and he'll take you to El Tigre to Oma's house." And there I was, almost on the plane that would take me back to Canada and I still hadn't called, or gone, or given out the parcels. Nothing.

After fourteen years of exile, I had gone back to Chile looking for those scents, voices, flavours, textures, and images that my memory insisted on calling "home." A tangle of old wounds had accompanied me during my six-week visit, as I ate my mother's *picante de albacora*, inhaled Guanaqueros' morning fog, listened to the roaring surf of the other end of the Pacific Ocean, crossed Calle Picarte on a Sunday at noon, and savoured a bowl of sea urchins with lemon juice and cilantro at the Valdivia wharf.

And now, arriving in Buenos Aires, I carried fresh wounds with me like baggage. The memory of the Andes as they had passed by the bus window on my way here was still huge in my mind; and walking down Florida and Lavalle, soaked in January sweat, I searched for my mother's face, the way I had left her, standing at the door of her Nuñoa house.

"Hello, yes, yes! We received the letter, we were expecting your call. Of course, we will be waiting for you at the station . . . around two o'clock? . . . We have a blue car." Wilma had told me that Uncle Otto had won it in a raffle twenty years ago. "Otherwise, we would've never been able to have one!" Aunt Ursula explains as we get into the impeccable Chevrolet, which up north would have already become a collector's item.

The house is only two or three blocks away. A small brick house, with red roof tiles. "Heat resistant," Uncle Otto explains. We hand out the parcels and sit down to have a few *mates*, while the patio burns in the mid-afternoon sun. Then we get ready to go to Oma's.

For Oma there is no parcel, but a cheque—to buy flowers. "Oma loves flowers," Wilma had told me. "My mom loves flowers," Uncle Otto tells me. On the way to El Tigre we stop at a flower shop and come out with a huge bunch of red and white roses. "She'll be delighted," Aunt Ursula says.

El Tigre, where the Paraná and Uruguay rivers become thick chocolate and give birth to the La Plata river. El Tigre, the northern tip of the Great Buenos Aires, with its working-class neighbourhoods and jasmine-scented corridors. Oma comes to the door. Oma looks exactly like Wilma, only that she is over ninety years old.

The hair, once blonde and straight, is now silver and bundled on the crown of her head. A firm chin, a thick and well-delineated mouth, just like Wilma's and repeated, once again, in Margot, her daughter. (*This same mouth in Germany? One hundred, two hundred years ago?*) The same big, restless hands and even the same eyes as Wilma's! (*Can that expression be inherited? Oma's mother? This grandmother's grandmother?*)

Oma looks at us, a little frightened, and then sees the roses. I give them to her, explaining that they have been sent by her son Federico and granddaughter Wilma, in Canada. She takes them and looks at me as if to say, "And they? Where are they?" She presses the flowers to her face, smells them and looks at me, while fat tears begin to roll down her cheeks. Then I know that Oma has not only lived for a long time, but that she has also carried her own heavy baggage with her.

"Friedrich," she says, with a German "r," even after more than sixty years of living in Argentina. "Wilma, when are they coming?" she asks. I hug her and explain that this time they were not able to come, but that they sent these beautiful flowers to her. "Very, very soon they will come to visit you," I say, knowing that I am lying. She knows it too, and smells the flowers while the tears continue to steam.

The house is shaded and inviting. The ground floor shelters an elaborate carpenter's shop, still intact, fifteen years after the grandfather's death. We go up the creaky stairs while Oma continues to talk, now in German. "When she's excited, she only speaks German," Uncle Otto explains. But because of one of life's miracles, I understand everything she says, even though I don't speak a word of German. I continue to admire the house, built by Oma and Opa, the carpenter, in the thirties, when they had just arrived from Germany, pushed out by the Great Depression.

The small living room is spotless, draped with crocheted curtains and furniture which has undoubtedly been crafted downstairs. The flowers find their place in a big vase. In an effort to act civilly, we sit down, thinking of the small talk we will engage in to fill the silences. But Oma has no time left for small talk, and little by little, she begins to weave Spanish into her speech. Uncle Otto and Aunt Ursula explain to me that she is senile, that she doesn't remember anything. They ask me to not pay attention to her; they apologize, explain. But I concentrate on listening to Oma.

They came in 1929, she tells me. On a big boat. There were people who died on the journey, particularly children. Friedrich was four then. In Germany there was no work, money was worth nothing. Then one day her husband said, "Ilse, we're going to Argentina to look for better times," and they left on the big boat full of immigrants.

Oma is not crying anymore. She just looks at me with an intense light that penetrates deep, because all of a sudden, sitting in this immaculate house in El Tigre, I realize that Oma's story is mine and that of my daughter's, who sits beside me. I look at Oma and I see so many exiled, immigrant women; women who left everything behind and learned to live again, who brought up their children in other lands and other tongues, always holding on to the increasingly fantastic memories of the faraway homeland.

"I never went back, never," Oma is saying now. "I never saw my mother, my father, my brothers and sisters again. We worked hard when we arrived in Argentina. We had three more children and little by little we built this house; there were many sacrifices. We never went back. All my children have a trade: Werner is a mechanic, Friedrich is a plumber, Otto is a roofer and Veronika is a secretary. We made it. We never went back. . . .

"And then one day Friedrich came to me and said: 'Mom, we are going to Canada. The situation here is very bad, we are going to Canada to look for better times.' What could I say? The situation here *was* bad. He already had a family of his own; it was his decision. In 1929 we came from Germany. The situation was bad. We never went back. Friedrich was four. He behaved so well on that boat, nothing happened to him. How many children does Friedrich have? Three daughters? Wilma is the oldest. Yes, I remember her."

That evening, walking along the bustling streets of Buenos Aires, it was not only my mother's eyes that I went searching for. There was also Oma's smile, as she stood at the door of her house in El Tigre, and the smiles of so many other women scattered around the world, standing at their doors, saying their hellos and goodbyes, in who-knows-what language, but with an accent all their own.

breaking the ice

Life lives itself, whether we like it
or not. Hope belongs to life, it's life
defending itself.

—JULIO CORTÁZAR

I FIRST ENCOUNTERED SIGNORA CARMELLA AND ROSA on the bleachers of the Britannia ice rink. That season, between September 1992 and April 1993, Signora Carmella's grandson and Rosa's son played hockey on the same team as my son. According to the minor league's rules, children were grouped by age, and each team had a name that reflected their age group. The year before they had been called "Atoms"; this season, they were called "Peewees"—the little ones. Every Wednesday, at six in the morning, we saw each other at Britannia, holding coffees in our shivering hands, while "the little ones," dressed as astronauts, got trained to hit a puck with a stick. From way inside, underneath my toque, scarf, boots, coat, and blanket, I would watch these children through the clouds of my own breath, as if watching the prolongation of one of my previous night's dreams.

In the distance I would also hear Signora Carmella's voice, the voice of a smoker, made up of explosions and pantings, like those steam locomotives that made the trip between Antilhue and Valdivia in the fifties, down there, in the south of Chile. It was already thirty-three years since she had come to Canada, Signora

Carmella said, but she wished she had never come. People here have no morals. You cannot keep your old country's values. Her daughter, who could have ever imagined anything like it, had had a child out of wedlock and now she, Signora Carmella, who had worked like a dog her whole life and deserved to be resting, had to help bring Enzo up, because if she didn't, who knows how this bambino would turn out. Thank God Enzo was a well-behaved boy, and so good at scoring goals. Maybe he would end up in the NHL, save the whole family from poverty, and in a few years she could finally rest in comfort.

But you never know in this life. How could anybody have guessed that her own husband would die only three years after coming to Canada? That he would leave her, just like that, with a small baby? And even though she had always been a housewife, she had had to get out of the house to clean other women's houses, and sometimes she even cleaned two a day and then cleaned her own, besides looking after her baby girl. Can you imagine? No relatives, nobody to help her. At the beginning she had thought she would work to get enough money to go back to Italy, but she never seemed to have enough and besides, where would she work in her hometown? As a widow, she would have to go back to living with her parents, and she had gotten used to managing her own money and her own affairs.

Once in a while, Rosa managed to get her stories in edgewise. Yes, when her husband had left her and the kids, she had had to go out of the house to work as well. What a coincidence. She had also cleaned houses until she found a job at Snazzie's, the clothing factory, which she still has. The salary is decent and she has some benefits; besides, she can retire when she turns sixty-five. Too bad it's still twenty-five years away, ha, ha, but at least she has been able to give her children a decent life, particularly considering that her jerk of a husband never showed up again.

Thank God the children have turned out quite fine. The *menina*, Luzia, is already sixteen and a very good girl, a loving daughter, happy to spend her time at home. Americo, the *menino*, worries her a little bit because he's twelve and already has a very strong character. Sometimes he becomes quite angry towards his father and says that he hates him, that he's going to go looking for him and that he's going to kill him because he left them, and she begs him not to do that, and then the poor boy breaks down and cries. At school she was told that the boy needs a male figure in his life. Somebody recommended that she register him at Big Brothers, that organization that gets an adult man to spend time with the boy, do something fun once a week. Life is so difficult, *meu Deus*, but in the Azores it would've been worse.

I could see the inevitable questions looming over me, getting closer and closer, and I waited for them inside my sheepish little world, trying to figure out how to take them, how to make them bounce off my woollen shield. What to say? Which tragedy to tell? The one about the military coup? The one about the two separations in Canada? The one about my daughter's father? The one about my son's father? The one about life as a banquet waitress at the Hotel Vancouver? Or the current one, about the psychologist, woman of colour, feminist, radical activist, Carlitos' mother, lover of a rather eccentric gringo? . . .

I'm from Chile, I said. I came twenty years ago, with my Chilean husband and my five-year-old daughter, the one that comes to the games sometimes.

Ah! Rosa said. That exotic girl is your daughter?

And what happened to her father? Signora Carmella asked.

Nothing, I said. He's around. We separated.

So, he's not Charlie's dad? Rosa kept pressing.

No, Charlie's dad lives in Toronto, I offered, trying to avoid another question.

Oh! both of them said at the same time, with circumspect expressions. And you haven't remarried? Signora Carmella insisted.

No, I laughed, I've had enough of men.

And that's as far as I went.

Every Wednesday we kept on seeing each other: me, as silent as I could be, and the two of them telling more and more tragedies: Signora Carmella with the incredible burden of having an irresponsible daughter and a grandson who was almost a teenager; Rosa, a single mother of two in the most difficult ages of their development.

I don't know what to do, Rosa said; it turns out that Luzia has been misbehaving, now she's come up with a boyfriend, a Negro boy, her classmate at Vancouver Tech. Can you imagine? Black as coal. *Preto, preto. Oh, meu Deus,* what have I done to deserve this? I found out that they have been fooling around for months! I didn't even know until last Sunday when Luzia and Americo had a fight because the *menino* wanted her to take him to the movies and she didn't want to and then Americo got angry and yelled at her that she didn't want to take him because she wanted to neck with her black boyfriend, and me, what are you talking about, my God. And the girl started to cry and yelled back to the boy that he wasn't even good enough to keep a secret, and me, what secret, and finally they tell me, can you imagine, Miss Silvia, you are a psychologist, tell me, what do you think?

Well, I tried to persuade her that there was nothing wrong with a sixteen-year-old girl having a boyfriend, and that if the boy was black, that shouldn't be a problem either. Signora

Carmella crossed herself the whole time I was speaking. I asked Rosa if she had met the boy and suggested that maybe she could invite him to their home, but there was no way she would listen. Signora Carmella didn't say a word. She kept on crossing herself.

At this point it was already November. At six a.m., mornings were not mornings but pitch-black nights and the rain felt like melted ice. Every Wednesday I brought my flask with coffee for three and Rosa showed up with homemade buns. Signora Carmella excused herself, saying that she couldn't eat so early in the morning, and dedicated herself to drinking coffee and smoking while exercising her tongue. A week after the story about the black boyfriend, Rosa didn't come to the practice and when I asked Americo about his mom, he said she wasn't feeling well. Signora Carmella had gone to get him and was going to take him back home. That morning the fog had wrapped its wetness around everything, and the cold soaked through to the bone. Signora Carmella was notoriously silent and she seemed to smoke with even greater dedication than on other days. I didn't know what to do. I gave her the mug of dark, steamy coffee and as I put it in her hand, the question just shot out of my mouth: What's wrong with Rosa?

Big sigh, puff, whorls of smoke, cough, and finally: She's sick in her soul. That bambina is going to kill her. Yesterday, she showed up at her mother's work, at Snazzie's, there on Third Avenue, with her black boyfriend. Right there, in front of all the women, the supervisor, everybody. And she yelled at her mother that if she didn't want to meet what's-his-name, she would have to anyway, because here he was, take a good look because this is my boyfriend. Then she yelled that she was going to leave home, that she couldn't take it any longer, that Rosa lived in the Middle Ages, that Canada was not the Azores, that her dad had been right in leaving her, and after all that, she just turned around and left. Just imagine, Silvia, she yelled all of this in English; *in English*. Everybody understood. Rosa called me last night. The supervisor had allowed her to leave early. Nice woman; I think she's Italian. So I went to her house, near Nanaimo and Twenty-Second Avenue. You know what? She lives in a basement suite. After all these years, she lives in a basement suite. . . . The thing is that she had a fever and she couldn't stop crying. Americo is a good boy. He was there, making tea for his mama and looking after her. I put a mint wrap on her forehead and she felt a little better. Just think: Luzia didn't go back home last night. Our poor Rosa is gonna die. That bambina is the apple of her eyes.

What to say? What to do? The psychologist in me should know, especially, what to say. Coffee, more coffee. Where is Rosa's bread? Rosa, Rosa, why did you abandon us on such an ugly day, when I was looking forward to eating your bread so much? I got used to thinking of my own mother's bread at six in the morning on Wednesdays. . . . It's been so many years since I last tasted it, and yours is so similar, who could've imagined it, when the Azores are so far from Chile. . . . Oh my God, what a difficult situation, I say. But, how can I be so stupid? Can't I think of anything else to say?

Signora Carmella, what do you think about this business with the black boyfriend? I ask at last. Do you really think it's so terrible that Luzia has fallen in love with a black boy?

I don't know, Silvia, Signora Carmella says. I don't know what to think. I had never seen a black person until I came to Vancouver, and it's only in the last few years that you see more of them. So, I don't know. . . . I've never talked to anybody who's black . . . Rosa hasn't either. Maybe if she talked to the boy. . . . That stupid Luzia! Why a black boy when there are so many Canadian and Portuguese boys? But they say that love is blind, right?

The same thing happened to my daughter Gina, she said, only

that the boy wasn't black. But when she was about that age, she fell in love with an Italian boy. She met him at the senior prom of the Prince of Wales High School, one of those rich people's schools near Arbutus. It was a blind date. Her friend Silvana had a Canadian boyfriend who used to go to that school, I don't know how she met him; a well-off family, I think the parents own some stores at the Pacific Centre. Well, the thing is that the boyfriend's friend didn't have a date and he was Italian, so Silvana thought that it would be great to ask Gina to go with him. They asked my permission well ahead of time; it was a dinner and dance at the Hotel Vancouver, where you used to work, everything paid for, on Saturday, June 26, 1979. I will never forget. My daughter was sixteen years old and she was very beautiful: tall, slender, blonde, hazel eyes. She's still good looking, but she gained weight with the baby. . . . I made her a velvet dress, the colour of ripe plums, you understand me, no? It turned out great. And I lent her my pearl necklace, the one that my husband gave me when we got married. She looked gorgeous! They came for her, Silvana with her boyfriend and this other boy, Antonio was his name—Antonio Fantinati. Gina didn't want to invite them in because she was embarrassed, you know, rich boys. So I said goodbye to her at the door. . . . I had also bought her a pair of Italian white leather high heels. I got them here, on Commercial, at Kalena's. And a matching purse. I know the owners of that store so they gave me credit and I paid for the shoes and the purse in three installments. Everything was sixty-five dollars and they didn't charge me interest. They're very nice. I'm sure that these days the bill would be over two hundred dollars!

And your daughter? she asks all of a sudden, taking me by surprise. Has she married?

No, but she lives with her boyfriend and in five months I'm going to be a grandmother! I hear myself say. I want to slap myself. What's Signora Carmella going to think? Like loose mother, like daughter? Why did I tell her this? And now that I've told her, how do I convince her that we are not "loose"? That for us marriage is not in our books anymore but that doesn't mean that we don't fall in love, that we don't commit ourselves to a relationship, that we don't love our children? What can I say to this Italian grandmother who has stuck to her values so desperately, who has suffered so much because of those values? How can I tell her about my abortion at seventeen, in a dark house on Seminario Street, near Bustamente Square in Santiago, all alone, far away from my parents, full of shame for having betrayed them so profoundly? Or about what happened to my girl when she was fourteen and a rapist attacked her in Central Park, her trauma, the long years of therapy, her encounter with this dark boy of South Asian ancestry who loves her and whom she loves? And now, they are going to give me a grandchild!

Can you imagine me as a grandmother, Signora Carmella? I almost explode everytime I think about it! Can you imagine Carlitos as an uncle? Oh, how we are going to love that child, how we are going to pamper that baby! We are going to bring him to the hockey rink and show him off to everybody. . . .

That's what I should've done with Gina, I hear Signora Carmella say in the distance. I should've let her go live with Antonio. His family threatened to disown him if he married Gina. Besides, as he was underage, he needed the parents' consent. After she got pregnant, he proposed that they live together, as if they were married. He said that he loved her and he wanted the baby. But I was completely opposed. How could I let my own daughter go live with her lover, just like that? My daughter was worth more than that! But thinking back, if I had let her live with him, maybe in time his family would've come around and accepted her. Especially after seeing the baby, Enzo. What a beautiful baby he was! Anybody would've wanted him as a grandson! But I fought to the death to stop her. Finally she didn't dare leave and stayed with me. In the end, Antonio got tired of fighting with me and waiting for her. He would come to visit her once in a while, and after the baby was born he was good, he helped with money, clothes, whatever he could. But finally he fell in love with somebody else, one of his own class. He's kept on helping, but he hardly ever visits. He's got other kids now, and poor Enzo seldom sees his father. I think that Gina is still in love with him. She never recovered from the blow. When he married that other girl, she was sick for several days; I thought she was going to die of heartbreak. If I had let them live together, more than twelve years ago, maybe we would all be happier now. Especially the bambino.

Tears run down Signora Carmella's soft, wrinkled cheeks. A long column of ash hangs from the end of her cigarette, ready to fall. The hand that holds the coffee mug is trembling, and a cough begins to shake her chest. I gently pat her back while I take the coffee mug from her left hand and the cigarette butt from her right. At the School of Psychology I was told never to get physical with a client. But why the fuck am I thinking about this? Signora Carmella is not my client! I put my arms around her and finally the locomotive in her chest explodes over my shoulder. As I cry with her, my face buried in her smoky coat, I realize that I am not only crying for this Italian grandmother, for Enzo and Gina, Rosa, Luzia and Americo. I'm also crying for all the accumulated tragedies of my own life, and for the trage-dies that my mother and my grandmother went through, and the tragedies my kids will go through, which we will never be able to avoid, no matter what. . . .

It's almost time to go. In silence, I pour Signora Carmella's last coffee. We have to go to Rosa's, I say.

Yes, we have to persuade her to at least meet the boy, no matter how black he is, Signora Carmella says. Yes. And we'll have to ask Americo to help us find Luzia.

We leave Britannia with the boys, their cheeks burning after an hour of sliding, skidding, slipping, falling, hitting and not hitting the puck with a stick, all of this on a surface made of ice. How strange life is! Signora Carmella and I are shivering, swimming in the cold fog. Uprising Breads Bakery, around the corner, is open. I go in and get a few buns, still hot from the oven, to take to Rosa's. For sure they're not going to be even close to hers, but this time there are more important things to worry about, at seven on a Wednesday morning in November in the east end of Vancouver.

bodily yearnings

Memory. My poison, my food.
—EDUARDO GALEANO

Disturbances in the night

WHEN THEY MEET, HE TELLS HER that he is Canadian to the marrow. To the marrow, she thinks. Where is the marrow? But, at that moment she is more interested in his clear eyes and his puppy-like hands than in his marrow. And why not admit it, she is especially attracted to the golden tangle of silky hair peeking out of his open shirt collar and to the boat-like rocking with which he moves. So, she decides to leave the question about the marrow for later. In case there is a later. And well, yes, there is a later.

That first conversation over a coffee is at 2:45 a.m., in the kitchen of the ninth floor of The Paradise building in downtown Vancouver. Both of them are employed by Pretty Maid Janitorial Services and work cleaning offices during the graveyard shift. They continue seeing each other at outrageous hours, between brooms and vacuum cleaners, mops and garbage bags.

The 2:45 a.m. coffee becomes a ritual and in her half-English she describes to him the crazy geography of her country and tells him silly stories about her childhood in Valdivia and her life as a university student in Santiago. He wants to know why she came to Canada, why she is here by herself, what happened to her family. . . . Then she tells him about the miners of the copper industry, the poor laundry women and the *campesinos*, the poets and the singers, the *alamedas* filled with dreams, and about a day of death in September: military marches, tanks, cries, terror. She explains that she was a student leader, that many like her disappeared and that her family, fearing for her life, insisted that she leave the country. Why Canada? he wants to know. Because, she answers with a shrug. It could've been Sweden, Holland. . . . But Canada took me in first, she adds with a twinkle in her eye. He lets himself be drawn by the light in her dark eyes and the bird-like movements of her hands, while he listens attentively and nods in silence.

He doesn't know exactly where Chile is, so on one of those nights, she brings a map and shows him the narrow strip of land sliding silently towards the Pacific at the other end of the world. *Chile es una larga y angosta faja de tierra*—Chile is a long and narrow strip of land, she recites in Spanish, grade one style, the way Miss Consuelo taught her. He caresses the map with the tip of his fingers as if wanting to feel the texture of the soil and the cool of the waters. He looks at her with curiosity, surprised perhaps that her mouth is capable of producing such a cadence of mysterious sounds. She tries to hold his eyes with hers, but an electric zig-zag runs through her back, and before he notices the red overflow that is coming up her neck, she gets up and runs to the washroom.

There, she cries in front of the mirror, her hands resting on the sink, the corners of her mouth turned down, her lower lip trembling imperceptibly. She washes her face with cold water and sits on the toilet sighing and humming, her hands extended over her womb, as if wanting to protect a wound, contain a pain. As if her whole memory were hidden in that warm and dark cavity, home to old mysterious inhabitants, spirits that cross borders, travel through entire continents, learn other languages. She stays there for a while, talking to her favourite phantom, the smallest one, the most intimate of all, and above all, hers. Hers forever. . . .

Phantom of the sea-refuge and the fish-child

I still remember you as a small beat in my womb, morning dizziness, nausea in grammar class. You had to exist so that the girl I was then could learn once and for all that life is sometimes purple, other times amber or translucent blue, but often grey, like fog. That there is a price attached to feeling a pair of hands under your skirt, a panting voice in your ear and damp grass at your back, a price paid with anguish, confusion, loneliness.

Ephemeral kiss coaxed into life, what could I do with your marine bud after the nocturnal stain on my skirt became bewilderment, chagrin? What could I do with my liver and my chest, full of birds?

Those sleepless nights I could feel you secretly growing in my refuge made of sea plants and salt, and I imagined you dark, like him, and perhaps with his big black eyes, but maybe with my mouth. The silence of my dormitory bed found me searching for you, talking to you, dreaming of the day that as a human you would push your head out and enter the world.

But I also thought of your grandmother, crying and crossing herself, and of your grandfather, silent and with a frown on his forehead, ready to explode like a bomb. Oh, just imagine how much talk there would've been by the neighbours, the milkman, the baker, the vegetable woman, the priest, and my godmother, if you had come into the world with your innocence and your *big eyes! . . . Who would've ever guessed she was always so special to her parents and now look at what she's done that's what you get from spoiling your children my God where is there some wood to tap on heaven forbid that's why I've kept mine on track from the beginning no boyfriends or anything like that see what happens this poor girl so young and to turn so crazy may God forgive her for this terrible sin I wonder who the jerk is. . . .*

And I, who believed in *la vie en rose*, walked through dirty alleys with a package of gauze and antibiotics under my arm, until I arrived at a black house. I never knew before that kitchens are not only for warming up our spirits and kitchen tables for preparing and sharing the food that gives us life. My back recoiled like a snail on the humid, cold surface. My heart said goodbye to you and my body prepared to die. . . .

Other wandering phantoms

He knocks softly on the washroom door and asks if she's okay. She gets up quickly as she says yes, not to worry, out in a sec. When she comes out, he is waiting for her, smoking a cigarette, his back resting on the wall. She feels stupid and ugly but, above all, vulnerable and exposed, as if she were naked. They walk back in silence to the kitchen. He puts the cigarette out in the glass ashtray on the counter, picks up the two cups with leftover coffee from the table and walks to the sink to wash them.

When she sees him standing in front of the sink, she feels invaded by great tenderness and the unstoppable need to get close to him, to nestle in the nooks of his body. She approaches him from behind and buries her face on his back while she circles his waist with her arms. It takes a while for him to get used to the wetness of her face on his back, the warmth of her belly on the curve of his butt. He covers her arms and hands with his own. She opens her eyes and sees her transgressing phantoms smiling at her from the kitchen door. Mauricio is there, with whom she used to make urgent and desperate love in the dark corners of the campus. Jaime, philosopher and basketball player, with enough resources to pay for a cheap hotel room in the Miraflores *barrio* once in a while. Claudio, comrade, friend and sweet lover, from whom she had to separate abruptly after the coup when he went underground and her parents sent her to Canada. And Carlos, her first love, looking at her from behind the others, offering her a toffee from the *Confitería Sur.* . . .

Phantom of the corridor

She searches in her memory and finds the phantom of her own face, the face of a girl with dark, round, surprised eyes. And when she listens to the girl laugh, she sees a set of big teeth and a mouth that splits open a mouse-face, clean and soft, covered with peach fuzz. She looks at her black school shoes and the blue socks that end at a pair of knees mapped by the marks of old scabs, attempting to hide underneath her starched white smock.

"I wonder what he saw in me at age twelve?" she asks herself now. The champion of flatness, her brother used to say to her. Flat in the front, flat in the back. All knees and teeth.

She knew that she liked all of him, but particularly his neck. She also liked certain clothes he wore, as if the clothes were part of his body. Her favourite was a coffee-coloured handmade sweater. Now she sees him in that sweater and a pair of blue jeans. She can't remember his feet, but she knows that his way of walking made her feel a certain longing in the pit of her stomach.

She had sent him a letter on a sky-blue sheet of paper, the only fine coloured kind that was sold at the ABC Bookstore. She had waited until she needed a new notebook for Spanish class and bought two sheets. Thank goodness her mom hadn't realized she had spent more than usual on the notebook. She had hidden the paper inside her Socials book and one night, after days of losing her appetite and sweating for nothing, she had stayed up, sitting in her bed, a candle for light, writing a letter to Carlos on the blue paper with the Parker 21 filled with purple ink that her dad had given her.

She hadn't told anyone about the letter, not even her best friend, because she knew that nobody would believe that she was going to take the initiative and declare her love to a boy. Not only would no one believe her, but they would also think she was crazy. A complete loony. Girls didn't do such things.

In the letter she had told Carlos that she loved him, that she liked his neck, his coffee-coloured sweater, everything. She had even talked about his way of walking and the longing she felt in the pit of her stomach when she saw him on the street. She had given it to him during math class, inside a book, her hand trembling. "Get the letter from inside and return the book to me," she had said in a hoarse voice that had sounded strange even to herself. He had taken the book like in slow motion, without understanding. "There is a letter, a letter for you, in the book. Be careful. Don't let anybody see it," she said, and rushed back to her desk, two rows up. A few minutes later she got the book back, without the letter.

She had spent the whole class with a stomach ache and the teacher had scolded her several times for not paying attention. That same afternoon, in Spanish class, he had left a piece of crumpled paper on her desk. The note said: "I'll see you after school at the *Confitería Sur*."

When she went into the candy shop, he was already there. She came up to him, sweating, and he gave her a small bag of toffees. They walked out in silence, while she opened the bag and put a toffee in her mouth. He was half a head taller than her and when she turned to look at him, the first thing she saw was his neck.

"Around the corner, on Camilo Henríquez Street, there is a house with a front corridor. Nobody will be able to see us and if we don't make any noise the people in the house won't even realize we're there," he said. She nodded, while she put another toffee in her mouth.

They walked to the house and went behind the corridor door. A crack of light came in from between the hinges. Her mouth was full of toffee and her ears were buzzing. They crouched down without saying a word and she felt for his mouth with her hands. She brought her own mouth to his, gave him the toffee she had left and went straight for his neck. She couldn't believe this was his neck, the one she had caressed from a distance with so much dedication. It was warm and soft and smelled of cinnamon, like LeSancy soap.

His hands had undone her braids and were now caressing her shoulders, her back. They kissed on the mouth and the toffee, much smaller now, came back to her. They got up and went out. He walked in one direction and she went in the other. She remade her braids in a hurry and ran her wet hands over her smock.

For several weeks she kept writing him love letters on sky-blue sheets of paper hidden in math, science, history and Spanish books. And for several weeks he replied with crumpled-up notes written on pieces of paper pulled from school notebooks. While she talked of skin, smells, eyes and stars, he gave her dates in the corridor of the Camilo Henríquez house.

Then, one day, the notes had stopped coming to her desk. She continued writing the blue letters for a few days, but he had grown tired of the corridor dates.

The kitchen table (revisited)

She gently frees herself of his arms and hands, and with her own hands begins to travel his body. She unbuttons his shirt and plays with the silky tangle on his chest. When her hands reach the zipper on his pants, he turns around slowly and takes her face in his hands.

He licks the salty tears that have wet her cheeks, kisses her on the eyes, nibbles her ears, and opens her mouth with his tongue. She plays with his penis and his buttocks. He frees her breasts, kneads them like fresh bread, and takes her by the waist. He seats her on the kitchen table and pushes her back gently with his chest, while he holds her head with one hand and fondles her pubis with the other one. The surface of the table welcomes her back. Her mind gets ready to resist, but her body surrenders to the embrace of this Canadian to the marrow with a taste of the ocean in his mouth.

Declaration of love in blue

My beloved John:
I recognize my mother in the long, dark hollow of your back. Let me wrap myself in the quiet of your skin and rest. The world is so big, it's so cold out there. Carry me inside your house of

murmurs and bones, the only one I have. My country existed such a long time ago; the blue of the ocean, the height of the snow, so far away. Southern rain, Macul in the fall, Valdivia river pushing life towards Niebla, Mancera.

My love, I have wanted you for so long, searched for you for so long. Now I'm here, in your corridor, in you. Don't let me leave.

Yolanda

Conversation in The Paradise

John: *(Holding her hands and kissing her on the neck)* I have something very special here in my pocket. . . . For you. . . . Want to see it?

Yolanda: *(Laughing and trying to stick her hand in his pocket)* What is it? . . . Let's see, show it to me. . . .

John: *(Stretching his right leg out so that he can get his hand in his pocket)* I hope you like it. . . . I mean, I hope you like the idea. . . . (He takes out a small box covered with wine-coloured velvet. His neck and his face turn almost the same colour as the box, his hand shakes, he feels sweat running down his back. He stands up and then kneels in front of her. He opens the box and takes out an engagement ring with a small diamond on top.) I want you to marry me. . . . I love you. . . . Do you want to marry me? . . . Please? . . .

Yolanda: *(Her eyes wide open, her face red as a tomato, the corners of her lips turned down, her lower lip quivering imperceptibly, sweat pearling her chest, her back)* John . . . oh, my God. . . . Nobody ever asked me to marry him before. . . . I never thought I would get married, know what I mean? . . . It's such a bourgeois thing to do. . . . What a beautiful ring! . . . Let's see. . . . Put it on me. . . . *(She stretches out her left hand. He slides the ring on her ring finger. It fits her perfectly.)* Is it a real diamond? . . . I've never seen a real diamond before. . . . Are you serious about wanting to marry me? . . .

Happy end

Advertisement in the classified section of the Vancouver Sun, *Monday, June 20, 1975:*

Yolanda Cárcamo and John McDonald are pleased to announce that yesterday, Sunday, June 19, they were married in a simple ceremony that took place at the Unitarian Church, 949 West 49th Ave., at 12:00 noon. The ceremony was followed by a reception attended by family and friends.

Guests who attended the wedding:

Mr. Arthur McDonald	Mrs. Margaret McDonald
Mr. David McDonald	Miss Marilyn Nichols
Miss Jessica Smith	Miss Wendy Young
Miss Diane Lacroix	Mr. Arthur Charles
Mrs. Mary Charles	Mr. Earl Denton
Mrs. Rosemary Denton	Miss Theresa Elliot
Mr. Glen Girard	Mr. Walter Halt
Mrs. Grace Halt	Mr. Bernard King
Miss Gloria Lee	Miss Brenda McIntyre
Mr. Brian de Souza	Mrs. Leslie de Souza
Mr. Dino Di Turi	Mrs. Francesca Di Turi
Mr. Rosendo Bahamonde	Mrs. María Cortez de Bahamonde
Mr. Gastón Gutiérrez	Mrs. Isabel Soto de Gutiérrez
Mr. Humberto Donoso	Mrs. Mercedes Osorio de Donoso
Miss Angélica Torres	Mr. Juan Morris
Miss Beatriz Olivares	Mr. Juan Manuel Meza
Mr. José González	Mrs. Hortensia Claro de González
Miss Adriana Moreno	Miss Wendy Valenzuela

Guests who were not able to attend the wedding but whose phantoms attended anyway:

Mr. Julio Cárcamo	Mrs. Mariela Oyarzún de Cárcamo
Mrs. Marta vda. de Cárcamo	Miss Rosario Oyarzún
Mr. Roberto Oyarzún	Mr. Carlos Lagos
Miss Gloria Cárcamo	Mr. Gregorio Cárcamo
Mr. José Manuel Cárcamo	Mrs. Laura Risso de Cárcamo
Mr. Juan Miguel Oyarzún	Mrs. Luisa Salgado de Lagos
Miss Marisol Pérez	Miss Mireya Torres
Miss Ana María Varela	Mrs. Elena Peña de Oyarzún

Phantoms who attended the wedding without being invited:

Fish-child

Yolanda-mouse-face girl

Jaime Betancur

Carlos Toro

Picarte Street

Camilo Henríquez Street

Municipal Stadium

Valdivia river

Macul Street

Villarrica volcano

Mancera

Mehuín

Plaza de Armas

Valdivia river boulevard

Kitchen table #1

Sea-refuge

Mauricio Rodríguez

Claudio Hormazábal

Sur Candy shop

Arnáiz Bakery

ABC Bookstore

Calle-Calle Bridge

La Alameda

Andes mountains

Niebla

Amargos

House on Yerbas Buenas Street

Miss Pilar (Spanish teacher)

The Paradise building

Kitchen table #2

Refreshments and banquet items:

Canapes, attention of Mr. Rosendo Bahamonde and Mrs. María Cortez de Bahamonde.

Stuffed turkey, attention of Mrs. Margaret McDonald.

Empanadas, attention of Mrs. Isabel Soto de Gutiérrez.

Barbecued meats, attention of Mr. Arthur McDonald and Mr. Humberto Donoso.

Chilean ensalada, attention of Miss Angélica Torres and Mr. Juan Morris.

Potato salad, attention of Mr. David McDonald and Miss Jessica Smith.

Green salad, attention of Miss Wendy Young and Miss Diane Lacroix.

Drinks:
Punch made with British Columbian red wine and strawberries.
Punch made with British Columbian white wine and pineapple.
Scotch on the rocks.
Labatt beer.
Coca-cola with Havana Club rum.

Cake:
Three-storey cake, combination of praline and *mil hojas*, filled
with *manjar blanco* and walnuts. Decorated with meringue, fresh
fruit and silver balls. Pillars between the second and third
storeys. Sugar-made bride and groom on the top. Attention of
Miss Beatriz Olivares.

Wedding waltzes:
Blue Danube
Antofagasta

The story continues

They go to live in a bachelor apartment in the West End, near the ocean and Stanley Park. Every night, when they come back from work, they fall asleep in each other's arms and when the noise of the traffic doesn't let her sleep anymore, she gets up in silence, makes herself a coffee and writes in the notebook she keeps for remembering life. While she writes, she watches him sleep, on his back, his right arm folded over his head, the hair on his chest escaping from between the sheets.

Inevitably, the words begin to open old drawers and let out smells and flavours, textures, sounds, streets, faces; certain ways of living life, of feeling, of being, so different from her present life. Phantoms. She submerges her whole body in this yearning for the past, her right hand dedicated to the difficult task of selecting, choosing, putting in linear order, and drawing small signs that she then reads and rereads until her body aches with so much longing.

When the pain doesn't let her breathe anymore, she gets back in bed. She takes refuge there, until she feels the pain give way to pleasure. Her body starts to melt slowly, molding itself to the warm nooks and corners of that other body, so different from hers, but now known inch by inch. The rhythm of love takes her to explosions of happiness, even peace. But once the pleasure recedes, the pain and the longing settle in each of her pores once again.

Many mornings, watching him sleep, she asks herself if she really loves him. He has become her lost home, her family, her friends. He is her country. Chile, the long and narrow strip of land sliding silently into the Pacific, now lives only in her past. But what will she do with all the wandering phantoms that don't let her live in peace? Will she ever be able to put them away in the drawers of oblivion once and for all?

Happy end (revisited)

The morning inundates everything with its scandal of birds and sun. The coffee warms her throat. The notebook for remembering life looks at her from the table. The telephone receiver makes its way to the curve of her neck and her index finger dials the number she memorized weeks ago.

"Canadian," a distant, impersonal voice answers in her right ear.

"I need to make a reservation," she hears her close, familiar voice say. "To Chile . . . yes . . . one ticket . . . no . . . one way only."

the labyrinths of love

AS A CHILD, I LET HER IN, probably too much. But at the moment of adolescence, I closed the door on her and she never came in again. Not even at the end. Her life's end, because I'm still here, wishing I had opened the door, but knowing that I always left her out.

She opened her door to me when she was about to leave. I went in to her through the dotted pink flannel nightgown that I lifted off her every day to wash the folds of skin, the nooks of flesh, the secret darkness of a body that she surrendered to me with no hesitation. She let me look at her, smell her, touch her, turn her over, unfold her, open her, feel her warmth on the tip of my fingers, wash away her odours with my soapy hands, moisten her with tears, know that she was soft, fallible, vulnerable, mortal.

I still don't know what to do without her. I don't have anybody to love me unconditionally anymore. Or maybe it's the other way around—I don't have anybody to love unconditionally anymore. Don't I love my children unconditionally? Aren't mothers supposed to love their children unconditionally? Or are the children the ones who have no alternative, the ones that love unconditionally?

The labyrinths of love. So much love.

Managua in August. Hot, sticky, heavy night. The taste of mud in my mouth. The television shows a group of captive politicians and their kidnappers getting ready for another sleepless night, while the floor under my feet dozes off, still warm, after the fiery heat of the day.

Nicaragua, a country where you can see history go by your window and touch it with your hand. A country where the street kids climb on the hoods of cars with sponges dripping dirty suds in the hope of earning a coin. A country where cardinals build Dantéesque cathedrals with mammary cupolas pointing to the sky while the shacks of the poor proliferate in the dirt all around them. A country that I come to and continue to come back to, stubbornly, wanting to find a dream come true, or a least the memory of a dream come true.

But while reality hits me, gets inside my pores, the television set opens up other worlds: limpid and clear, worlds with no garbage, no thirty-year-old women who look twice their age, worlds with running water and sewage systems. Worlds with people who eat and sleep, love, betray, feel, hug, laugh, cry. People who live.

Tonight, it's the world of *El Pantanal*. The natural beauty of the Brazilian southern Matto Grosso takes over the width of the screen, filling it with textures and sounds. Nature serves as a frame for the feelings of intense characters, capable of seducing even the most skeptical spectator. I have no problem letting myself be seduced by the mouths of these beautiful people who modulate in Portuguese but are heard in a rather strange Spanish. So what? I think, while I let myself sink into this colourful story, populated with fiery lovers, sun-warmed bodies, perfect smiles, juicy barbecues, songs, horses, rivers, and women who become jaguars.

In the few times that I have watched the program I have become fond of María Marruá, an intelligent woman of extraordinary integrity and a strength that even the best guerrilla fighter would want for herself. I am also fascinated by her daughter, with her long dark hair and a hardness in the face that does not interfere with her profound beauty. But tonight, I cry the death of María Marruá at the hands of a cowardly bad guy. The daughter finds María Marruá dead in the river. She takes her in her arms and cries. She cries on the screen. I bawl my eyes out in the hot reality of this Managua night.

The phone rings. Long distance from Vancouver, Canada. My aunt is trying to get hold of me. My mom has lung cancer. The doctor has given her a year to live. My mom is going to die. I'm going to take her in my arms, like María Marruá's daughter, and I'm going to cry. We will not be in a river, in the Brazilian Pantanal, but in the Quillota house. My mom will not be the beautiful, strong, young woman that María Marruá was. No, she will be seventy-five years old and she will be very, very weak. She will not become a jaguar, either. Regarding myself, especially myself, I will not look at all like María Marruá's daughter, that precious young thing. Instead, I will be forty-six years old, short, pudgy, with glasses. Besides, it will be real. It will not be a TV soap opera. My mom will die for real.

My mom's cakes. Round, square, rectangular, tall, low, with several layers. Coconut Foam, Primavera, Fantasia, Genovesa, Imperial Vienna, Black Forest, Musselina, Borrachita, Carnival, Hildelberg, Moccha. My mom, arriving at the Vancouver airport with a huge package in her hands. Hildelberg cake for her granddaughter's birthday. Hildelberg cake, all the way from Quillota, Chile. A taxi, a bus, another bus, another taxi. An international flight. Electronic check-up at the Santiago airport. Immigration and customs at the Vancouver airport. My mom arrives in Vancouver on her granddaughter's birthday and hands her her present: the huge Hildelberg cake. Our surprise surprises her. It was simple: she explained that she hadn't seen her granddaughter for a long, long time and that she had brought her a cake, made with her own hands, as a birthday present. Nobody gave her any problems.

In this picture she must be nineteen. My brother is probably one and my dad, twenty-five. Santiago, a photography studio on Ahumada Street, near the Plaza de Armas. Maybe at the Portal Fernández Concha. Winter of 1938? Her second wedding anniversary? Or maybe March of that year? My brother's first birthday?

She must have made my brother's outfit. Beehive stitch, long-sleeved turtle-neck sweater, three little buttons on the shoulder. Short pants. Patent leather shoes. White ankle socks. The boy's hair is combed back with gel. Undoubtedly, my mother's hands. My dad's hair is also combed back; his own hand. Double-breasted jacket, a tie for the picture. White shirt; my mother's hands.

She was always proud of her hands. "Working hands," she

would say. When I was a kid, I wanted her to have the hands of a lady, like the mothers of the rich kids, or my aunts' hands: white, slender, soft, with long fingernails, painted red or pink. "That shows that they don't do anything all day," she would say.

One of her hands is holding the child; her left hand, a wedding band shining on her ring finger. Her other hand is resting on her lap. Most likely she also made the dress that she wears. Bunched-up short sleeves, pointy collar, pleated bodice, and buttons running down the front. Straight skirt covering her knees. Nice legs. She was also proud of her legs: "Better to have rounded legs than broomsticks," she would say. What happened to the serenity of this immense smile? I never knew her like this, emanating happiness, peace. This is my mother. This beautiful young woman is my mother.

This is my mother. Seventy-four years old. She has shrunk so much that now she is shorter than me. Her face has the softness and texture of an old map. It's difficult to find the young woman in the 1938 photograph in this face. The smile is still wide, but the eyes have become smaller and reflect pain. Her body has been invaded by cancer. The cough doesn't let her sleep. She doesn't want to eat anymore. But the pain is older and deeper than the cancer. Pain. Twenty years without her children and grandchildren. "It hurts to know that they grew up so far away from their country," she told me on the phone when I called to tell her I was coming. "It hurts to know that they speak another language, have other values."

She asks me to gather all her recipe notebooks. We go through them together as she marks them: very good, good, acceptable, not good. Maybe this is her most important legacy. On September 18, Independence Day, I make *empanadas*. It takes me the entire day. I cut my left middle finger chopping onions, I burn my right forearm on the edge of the oven, I sweat, my feet hurt. The recipe had been marked very good, but after so much suffering the *empanadas* turn out only acceptable.

Her other legacy is her art. Tiny clay flowers in all possible colours. Children, animals, witches. Miniatures, kneaded and painted by my mother's working hands. Old women made of old stockings. Silk hair, embroidered eyes and mouths, rouge on their cheeks, tiny leather booties. Years of work in the dining room-workshop of the Quillota house. The creatures that have come out of her hands fill every possible surface: shelves, sideboards, cupboards, chests of drawers, curios, sidetables, windowsills. They are an army, though different from the one that pushed her to mould creatures with whom to share her solitude.

I have to tell the children about Chile, she tells me. I must not let them forget about their roots, their origins. When she's awake, she can't stop talking. She tells me again and again about my grandparents, her youth, the Chilean north when she was a child, the five hundred year anniversary of the foundation of Valdivia, the resistance of the Mapuche: "They never surrendered," she tells me. I manage to borrow a tape recorder. Is she going to let me record her stories? "It's for your grandchildren, your great-grandchildren," I say. "So that they can hear you, listen to the family stories in your own voice." "Okay," she says. She keeps on telling and telling. "Tell me about how you met my dad," I ask. "That was a long time ago," she says and cries. I turn the tape recorder off.

It's clear that she's decided to die soon. One year is too long. Yesterday she asked me when the return tickets are for. "In two weeks. But we're coming back for Christmas," I say. "No, too much expense," she replies. Tony, my Canadian companion, asks her if she wants the outside of the house painted. She's ecstatic. For Tony, it's a way of showing her his love; besides, it gives him something to do, to busy himself outside, in the open air. She wants to leave her life in order.

She gives me precise instructions on what to do with everything. Obviously, it is my responsibility since I am the only daughter. The pottery and the dolls have to be fairly distributed among family and a few friends. The knitting machine is for Prudencia and the sewing machine for Gloria. "At least they will have a way of supporting themselves if their husbands leave them or die," she says. The furniture has to go to family members according to need. And the house is for whoever in the family needs it. Above all, I must make sure that nobody fights for any of the material things she is leaving behind. I don't want to remind her that it will be difficult to fight, because we can take neither the furniture nor the house back to Vancouver.

She takes refuge in her bed. She doesn't want to go to the hospital. It's hard for her to breathe and she has to be helped when she wants to turn over, sit up. Her head aches a lot, she has nausea. She doesn't vomit; she hasn't eaten anything for many days now. The doctor says that the cancer has also invaded her brain. When she's awake, she keeps on telling stories. Sometimes she cries. I comb her hair, fan her with a piece of cardboard. Every day I cut a camellia from the little tree in the backyard that for some miraculous reason decided to light up early in the season. I put the red flower in a small vase on her night-table and she smiles.

My brother, his children, my daughter, begin to arrive from Canada. At least we are all here. When my father died nine years ago, the dictatorship didn't let us into Chile. He died without his children and grandchildren. My mother is surrounded by warm bodies that take turns keeping her company.

My daughter helps me sift through the quantities of objects, books, toys, clothes, letters, photographs. My mother kept everything we couldn't take to Canada. And in her fifty-seven years as a housewife, she never threw anything out. Environmentalists would give her a gold medal for not polluting the planet. Here is the brown dress she wore in the picture from 1938. Moths have eaten a great deal of the cloth. The same with my brother's sky-blue outfit. Here are the photographs, our own old toys. This dress was my first party dress. My mother made it for me and I still remember the pins on my skin when I had to stand motionless for hours on a chair while she took it in here, let it out there. Oh, how I hated her while she made me that damned dress! She probably hated me too.

My mother dies at noon on a Friday. I'm the only one sitting by her bed, reading Amy Tan's *The Kitchen God's Wife*, while I hold her hand. The previous night I noticed that the palms of her hands were black and blue, as if she had bruised them somehow. I noticed because she had her hands in front of her eyes and she was moving them gracefully, as if she were a flamenco dancer. She was looking at them because they had already begun to die. What's the sense in living if your hands die?

Everybody is around, in the dining room, in the kitchen, in the back rooms, in the backyard playing with the dog. Tony sticks his head in the door and says in English: "Finished. The house looks great," and goes to the bathroom to wash up. I lift my eyes from the book and look at my mother, whose chest grows with every effort she makes to get some air into her lungs. I squeeze her hand and say: "*Mamita*, the house looks beautiful." She opens her eyes and looks at me. Her eyes have changed colour, or maybe death has also got into her eyes. Her chest deflates. Yes, it deflates. My mother stops breathing.

She had told me how to dress her: the black dress, the older one of the two she owned, because it would be a waste to use the newer one. Somebody may want it. The black shoes and the black knee-highs, but without the elastics because they are too tight. She didn't say anything about the undergarments, so I try to guess what she would like. One of the sleeves in the black dress is a bit torn. I mend it carefully. She would never forgive me if I sent her to the tomb in a torn dress. I polish the black shoes. With the skillful precision of a surgeon I take the elastics off the knee-highs, making sure I don't start any runs. I comb her hair softly and I put a small bunch of her own clay flowers on her chest. So much love.

I still don't know how she met my father. I will never know how she met my father. But now I know that I loved her unconditionally, in spite of not having opened the door.

The labyrinths of love. How will I live without this love?

a balanced diet: laughing and crying at the house in the air

Going to school was forbidden
going to university was forbidden
constitutional rights were forbidden
all sciences, except for military science,
were forbidden
the right to protest was forbidden
the right to question was forbidden
that's why today,
so that it never happens again
I say to you, brothers and sisters,
forgetting is forbidden!

—RUBÉN BLADES

I HAVE JUST EMERGED FROM THE DESERT: salty, hot, undulating, granulated recumbent skin facing an infinite extension of blue. I am greeted by a series of green explosions grooved by slithering mountain waters: Huasco, Elqui, Limarí, Choapa, Petorca, Aconcagua. The pulse of the Pacific Ocean has kept me company along the way and I have let go of its embrace of froth to journey through orchards and gardens until finally arriving at the madness of Santiago.

The snow-capped peaks of the Andes float in the middle of the sky, suspended there as if by magic. The city takes me in its cloud of waste, punctuated by noises of metal and flesh, screeches, horns, shouts, bells, vendors of chewing gum, band-aids, needles, handkerchiefs, Christmas ornaments. Here is the centenarian railroad station, a rejuvenated shelter for artists. Over there, *La Vega*, the open market with its mountains of peaches, grapes, chirimoyas, tomatoes, avocados. A little further, the colourful food kiosks with their open-pit fires and makeshift dining areas full of working people laughing and eating.

My mouth waters at the thought of a succulent *caldillo de congrio*, white fish chowder, *pastel de choclo*, corn casserole, or *porotos granados*, fresh bean stew. I walk over and mix in with the crowd. The ambrosial aroma of cumin seed and basil fills my body with pleasure. I haven't had *porotos granados* for a long, long time, I say to the smiling woman dressed in an immaculate white smock. Enjoy it, *señorita*, she says as she hands me the steaming bowl. It's good for you. A very balanced dish: protein, veggies, a little bit of fat, not too much, and spices to make you happy. Besides, it'll keep your digestive system going for a while, she adds with a chuckle and a sparkle in her eyes. I sit at a table already occupied by a dozen or so people and eat in silence as I smile and listen to the jokes and to the once familiar sounds of the *barrio*. The only thing missing is the voice of the trains that twenty years ago departed daily for Valparaíso with their first, second, and third-class cargoes.

The spotless metro offers me waves of Chileans coming from names where a long time ago a big hand took me across the Alameda or a mouth tenderly kissed my neck: Universidad de Chile, Santa Lucía, Baquedano. La Moneda is something else; that's where a good part of my life was bombed.

I come out again into the city turmoil under one of those ruthless Santiago summer suns. The tide of bodies carries me among vehicles determined to put an end to my precarious humanity. My heart has changed in all these years. Not only do tears well up at the slightest signal, but everything seems to scare me. I have also lost the bullfighting skills that I learned so well when I was young. But I do succeed in getting to the other side safe and triumphant and I hasten towards Bellavista. In those days, there was no Bellavista quarter. The only ones who had taken note of its existence were the white, mute statue of the Virgin Mary on top of San Cristóbal Hill, the inhabitants of the old neighbourhood houses, and Neruda, contemplating the city with his eyes of a poet from *La Chascona.*

The Mapocho river runs along, skipping rocks and sand mounds. I stop for a few seconds on the Pío Nono bridge with the Andes at my back. No, this time the river is not carrying mutilated corpses in its chocolate water. There aren't even scraps of paper or tin cans floating in the current, the way there used to be. Santiago has become a very clean city. As clean as oblivion.

Santiago, August 27, 1993

My dearest Laura:

I can't believe that I found you after all these years! Somehow I knew that you had ended up in Canada, but my understanding is that Canada is a very, very big country, so. . . . When I learned you were in those cold faraway lands, I began to imagine you dressed in a suede jacket with a big fur-trimmed hood and sealskin boots, riding a sled pulled by six dogs with blue eyes. Like good *gringos* (ha, ha). I even did a painting with this image. I placed you in what I picture as the Arctic, everything white and luminous. I laughed a lot because as a consequence of that painting, the critics spoke of my mystic tendencies, of the surrealist influences, etc., etc. I just let them speak. What else could I do? Of course nobody knows (but now I'm telling you) that this painting only represented my efforts to keep you alive in my memory.

Since I knew that you were in that great northern country, I have been asking everybody who seems to have a connection up there about you. That's how I learned the names of many Canadian places, some of which sound extremely interesting to me. The one I have liked the most is Saskatoon. I don't know why, but it sounds like something big and very red, although from what I was told, most of the time it is rather white. . . . But now I also know that not all of Canada is like a refrigerator; in fact, some parts are more like a freezer (ha, ha).

About two years ago I met a Canadian woman who told me that she had read a book you published in Toronto. My hair almost fell off my head. I asked her everything I could think of, but the *gringa pelotuda* didn't remember much and seemed to know nothing, particularly about where you lived. She said she would send me the book, but until this day. . . . She probably thought I was a bit crazy.

I had been trying for so long to find you that I had almost lost hope when this plump elderly fellow wearing grey flannel pants with elastic suspenders came up to me during the last exhibition I did at La Casa Larga and started talking. I can't even remember how it was that he mentioned that he lives in Canada. Automatically I asked him if he knew Laura Arzola and then I heard him say yes, the writer, and I told him she's a great friend of mine! (I never lost the conviction that in spite of our long separation you would continue being a great friend of mine. . . .) I haven't seen her for twenty years, I told him, and then he said, I'm going back to Vancouver next week and if you want I can take her a letter.

So, I've been thinking about you non-stop since that day and I've been remembering things and waking up in the middle of the night trying to imagine your face and body now that you are twenty years older, and then two nights ago I had to get up and paint you. This time you were not in the white Arctic but in a gigantic green forest because *don* Luis, the fellow who is taking you the letter, told me that the Vancouver landscape is just like the south of Chile. In the painting you are walking in the forest, naked, with a basket full of homemade bread on your arm, a basket just like the one the country woman had that day in Valdivia, a few days after the coup, when we went to visit the political prisoners and we learned about Mario. . . .

That morning the mud came up to our ankles. We had crossed the choppy river in the usual boat and we arrived at the doors of the prison soaked in rain. About fifty people were already waiting for visiting hours to begin. We armed ourselves with patience while we settled in the line-up, you with your usual humour, telling jokes to pass the time and hide the tension, me with a knot in my stomach. After a few minutes the rumour exploded like dynamite: twelve prisoners had been executed the night before, among them Alejandra, Fernando, Miguel, Arcadia, and Pepe. You said that it could not be true, that they would not go that far. The international observers are already here, you said. They can't kill a dozen young people just like that.

We waited in the torrential rain of the south, that furious, patient rain that makes ferns grow everywhere. No one spoke, some cried. But not you. Head high, you told me that the military would never see Mireya Jiménez cry. Inside the prison were my *compañero*, other friends and comrades. But, were they? I raised my head, straightened my shoulders, and tried to imitate you, but hot tears hopelessly slid into my mouth.

The line began to advance slowly at the rhythm of padlocks and chains, gates opening and closing. Some went in, others came out. And then we saw her. The country woman dressed in black with a basket of bread under her arm. Two women held her by the arms and practically dragged her to a tree. There they sat in the mud and the woman with the basket began to scream and cry with the bread still intact in her basket.

They had shot her son. It's true, you said. They killed them.

The line continued to move lazily. We got to the gate. I couldn't hear or feel anything anymore, only the loud thudding of my heart and the nausea in the pit of my stomach. You, pale but unshakeable. Good morning, corporal, good morning, ladies. Come in. Arms locked, we walked to the visiting shack. I slipped in the sticky mud, twisted my ankle. Don't surrender, you said.

The shack smelled of b.o. and cigarettes. A smoke cloud enveloped the thin and emaciated silhouettes of the prisoners. I looked for Mario in his usual spot, but somebody else was there. I tried to find him in each one of those wasted faces, but I only found eyes extended towards me like arms. The vomit came out of my body in the same instant that I realized that Mario was one of the executed ones. Everything became an immense black stain sprinkled with coloured lights. I heard your voice asking me to help you get me out of there. I still remember your hands under my arms, taking me back to the street. Almost like flying.

The rain, the trees, even the people's faces had acquired an exceptional clarity. I floated down the street while I watched the transparent perfection of the veins on the leaves, complete maps growing out of whispering trees, the crystal-like quality of the raindrops filling the resplendent space, dark fears framed by eyelashes on faces carved in stone. Your voice took me out of my dream. The prisoners had told you that the twelve had died like real revolutionaries. When they were taken out of their cells, they left singing "The International" at the top of their lungs and soon the others joined them from their own cells. They were still singing when they heard the commands and the shots.

I felt the mud get into my shoes and the rain soak my neck while my voice escaped from my chest in a torrent. When we turned the corner you hugged me, your face warm with tears. They will pay for it, the fucking assholes, you said. They will pay for it.

Vancouver, September 9, 1993

Dearest Mireya:

You have no idea how moved I was by your letter. Of course it also unleashed a deluge of nostalgia and memories and I haven't been able to stop thinking about you and all of those who were part of my life back then. But instead of getting up in the middle of the night to paint, I have been getting up to write.

Mireya, you will never stop being a great friend of mine, in spite of the distance and the years. When two people have spent so many great and terrible times together, it is impossible to cut the connection. Besides, without your strength and your help, I would've never been able to live through so many blows and sorrows.

But life continues and somewhere we always find the desire to keep on living. I arrived in Buenos Aires on December 13, 1973, that is to say more than two months after you and Carlos helped me jump over the fence of the Argentinean Embassy in Santiago. My mom and the girls arrived just before Christmas. I managed to get a tiny apartment in El Once, a Buenos Aires neighbourhood. We lived there for eight months, until we got the permit to come to Canada as refugees.

Buenos Aires is a fascinating city and Argentineans were very good to us. Besides, there were an impressive number of exiled

Chileans, so we always had friends visiting and helping us to remember and bitch. In general, we managed to survive, although for several months I was in a deep dark pit. I couldn't come to terms with the fact that Mario had been killed, that they had amputated our dreams overnight, that we could not go back to Chile until who knows when. . . . You know how much I enjoy my food (I still do) and how I was always so adamant about having a balanced diet (I still am). Well, during our stay in Argentina, I lost over twenty pounds, and not because I went on a diet. I just couldn't eat.

My mom was as strong as a rock. She was not only very supportive to me but also became the girls' mother, father, and grandmother. She took on all of the housework while I worked downtown as a secretary in a lawyer's office. That allowed us to survive barely, but to survive after all. Somehow my mom made ends meet and kept the girls well-fed and healthy.

We arrived in Vancouver on August 7, 1974, and began to live again, this time in a different language. At the beginning the government supported us and sent me to English classes. After a few months, my mom began to work cleaning people's houses and I got a job as a banquet waitress in a fancy downtown hotel. Here you have material for another oil painting; try to imagine me in a waitress uniform: black dress, white apron, bonnet and gloves, carrying a round tray with fifty (filled) glasses over my shoulder, serving drinks to an army of jerks, businessmen dressed in thousand-dollar suits. The tables are full of fancy food: caviar and asparagus canapés, smoked salmon, goose liver paté, camembert and black grapes, twenty-seven kinds of cream crackers. . . . Then I trade my drink tray for one with platters of steak and lobster, coq-au-vin, *insalata primavera*. . . . What do you think? Are you impressed? My only problem was that I couldn't touch any of these extraordinary gastronomical creations until the banquet was over and all the waiters and waitresses sat down in the kitchen to eat leftovers. So, can you find a way of working my hungry eyes into the painting?

In 1976 I went back to university to study Literature because I realized that my Chilean degrees would never be recognized here. We lived in a cute little white house in the student housing complex on campus. After the basement suite in the city, it felt like a mansion. I worked as a teaching assistant in the Latin American Literature Department and that allowed us to live quite decently for a few years. The girls really enjoyed living in that complex because there were lots of kids in the neighbour-hood and their school was great.

That year I fell in love again. Yes, I have loved again and although it was difficult at the beginning, I succeeded in saying goodbye to Mario and getting on with my life. Of course he will always have a special place in my soul. Besides, he is my daughters' father, and we have kept his memory alive not only because of everything he meant to us personally, but because his life and assassination cannot be forgotten: they are part of our history and of Chilean and world history. I know that this sounds rhetorical twenty years later, but these are words that I feel very deeply. Besides, from a personal point of view, I have to come to terms with the fact that even if I wanted to forget, I can't. I do have a mind and a body to remember with. Forgetting is not an option.

During those first years in Canada we, the Chileans, together with many Canadians, organized a large solidarity movement. Our days were filled with different kinds of activities: political events, *peñas*, concerts, marches. Imagine that I even learned how to make *empanadas*! You know that I never made them while I lived in Chile, but here I had to learn and not only that, I had to learn how to make five hundred at a time! Also, in 1978,

I was part of that world-wide hunger strike in support of the relatives of the *desaparecidos* in Chile. Remember? Those certainly were memorable days. . . .

Two hundred cups of flour fifty cups of shortening warm water lots of warm water buckets of warm water salt baking powder it has to be Royal because it's the best other ones are crap thank goodness here in Canada you can buy Royal just like in Chile . . . *hunger* . . .

Mix and knead knead knead knead knead knead knead until the dough is soft and firm chop lots of onion lots and lots of onion in small small cubes chop chop chop many onions so many that even if you're really crying everybody will blame the onions and you can say things like these onions are so strong so strong while you cry your eyes out but make sure you have a hanky to blow your nose because *empanadas* with tears and snot may upset the public's stomach . . . *hunger* . . .

Crush garlic lots of garlic heads crush them crush them crush them fry everything in lots of shortening until it's golden mmmmmm good good I wonder how the mothers of the disappeared are doing in Chile I wonder if they are *hungry* like me or maybe when they think of their disappeared children they don't feel *hungry* anymore maybe I shouldn't be feeling *hungry* but what can I do when I'm starving I have to breathe deeply and drink lots of water lots of water that's what the doctor said lots of water I'm up to here with the damn water. . . .

Add the ground beef lots of ground beef kilos and kilos of ground beef *hunger* oh my God why did I ever get involved in this mess what do I know about *hunger* strikes but why am I thinking like this this is completely anti-revolutionary shut up

Laura think about the disappeared their mothers their relatives their friends think of other people your daughters your mother don't only think of yourself . . . *hunger* . . .

Yes I'm better now I'm not so *hungry* anymore it was just a moment of weakness you have to roll the dough until it's quite thin but not too thin because then the *empanadas* will break so you cut rounds of flat dough don't forget the raisins and the olives here they have pitted olives which is great because then you don't have to break a tooth every time you eat an *empanada*. . . . Bake them for a good forty minutes until they are golden brown . . . *hunger* . . .

Rosita says that they're organizing a *peña* for the weekend they're expecting lots of people and they want the *hunger* strikers to speak I don't know the last few days I've been very sleepy all I want to do is sleep and sleep it feels strange I'm not *hungry* anymore people come visit us and we ask them what did you eat for dinner tonight and they don't want to tell us and we laugh and insist come on tell us what you ate and they feel bad and we keep on bugging them until they tell us meatloaf with mashed potatoes roast chicken with rice and we say mmmmmm that sounds good but the truth is I'm not *hungry* anymore and I say mmmmmm just to say mmmmmm because I'm expected to say mmmmmm but I actually don't feel anything and I only want them to leave so that I can go to sleep. . . .

The *peña* is next Saturday at the Ukrainian Hall and Pato and myself will speak we have to get our speeches ready in Chile there are more than two thousand *desaparecidos* disappeared people captured by the secret agents of the dictatorship who never turned up again there are testimonies of political prisoners who saw them in concentration camps or torture houses and then never again never again their relatives demand an explanation and at this very moment in Chile they are on an indefinite hunger strike until they get an explanation we are showing our solidarity with them and from exile we join them until final victory *compañeros*. . . .

Everybody is clapping their mouths full of *empanadas* the kids are running around in between the tables soon they will get on stage to sing *Duerme Duerme Negrito*, *La Petaquita*, *De Colores*, the *zampoñas* and *quenas* sound so beautiful I feel like a sleep-walker having this glass of water my younger daughter is falling asleep on my lap she will not be singing tonight with the other kids I wish I could just go back home tonight with my daughters and my mom but from here I go back to the Unitarian Church to go on with the hunger strike. . . .

They are negotiating some agreements last night we called the Vicariate of Solidarity in Chile it looks like the strike will be over tomorrow we'll go to the consulate at noon my mom says she'll make me chicken *cazuela* sounds good but I don't feel a thing I could just not eat for the rest of my life I wonder what would happen if I didn't eat anymore for sure I would die. . . .

What's it like to be dead Mario I still miss you so much but it's different now it's not in that desperate way anymore now I can talk to you without crying and tell you about our girls so precious who said I could talk to you without crying I just said it oh well yes I still cry and probably I will cry for the rest of my life. . . .

His Highness the Chilean consul will not talk to us we are going up the stairs in the consulate building and he's closing the door on our face the TV cameras are here everything will be on tonight's news the demonstration is quite big for a Monday at noon from here I go back home what will it be like to eat again after fourteen days of only water? . . . I wonder how the relatives of the disappeared are feeling after this first little victory but you could never get over something like this your loved ones vanished forever what did they do with them at least we're alive and some day we'll be able to go back when when. . . .

Santiago, October 31, 1993

Laura, Laura, Laura:

I'm about to explode with happiness. I've been floating since I got your letter saying that you're coming. . . . I got in touch with your brother in Valdivia and they can't wait for you, or rather all of you, to get there. I'm dying to meet your *gringo* in person. I don't know why I'm calling him *gringo* because in the picture he looks more Mexican than *gringo*. I found it amusing that he was born in Oxford to parents born in India. You have always been so creative that now you got yourself a Canadian Pancho Villa of South Asian ancestry, born in Oxford! Does he drink tea at five o'clock in the afternoon with his pinky poised like the queen?

The girls look beautiful with their Arzola smiles. Of course they are not girls anymore but grown women with their own lives and their own *gringos*. . . . But again, I don't understand anything, all these *gringos* seem to be from anywhere except Gringoland. Both the boyfriends are very good-looking. The one with the Italian parents definitely looks like a Roman Apollo and the one with the Ukrainian grandparents looks more like my idea of a gringo: blonde and blue-eyed. I will have everything ready to have a United Nations meeting when everybody gets here (ha, ha).

I think it's an excellent idea that you come first and everybody else joins you later. That way we'll have time for our own little reunion. I also think it's great that you have decided to fly to Lima and from there to Arica so that you can come down the desert by land. The desert is very impressive. Three years ago I went to San Pedro de Atacama for the first time and I was fascinated. Since then I have gone back several times and have painted a whole desert series which has been shown in different galleries with quite a bit of success. The idea was not only to show the desert as landscape, but also as the setting for the atrocities of Pisagaua, San Pedro, and all the places where they have found remains of the disappeared.

I cried a lot when I read that your mom died without having been able to come back to Chile. It must've been very painful for her and all of you. I think it's incredible that she wouldn't be allowed to come back just to die in her own country. The hatred and inhumanity of the military go beyond belief. But I'm glad that at least your brother was able to go to Canada to be with her, you, and the girls during her last days. It will be an honour for me to go to Valdivia and join the family in the ceremony to disseminate her ashes. There will be no better resting place for *doña* Nati than the majestic Calle-Calle river.

I'm living up in El Arrayán, in a quaint little house on the foothills of the Andes. I have a studio with lots of light and a view of the Mapocho valley. The yard is a series of terraces where there are fruit trees, flowers, and I have even got lettuce and tomatoes! You'll love it. The only problem, or perhaps it's a blessing, is that it's quite far from the centre of town. So, I think that the most sensible thing is that we meet in Bellavista. There is a nice café called The House in the Air. . . .

The administrative employees of the University of Chile's Law School have surrounded the building with placards: We deserve decent salaries, the School will not function without us, the placards say. I walk by briskly and smile. I hope at least one of them may have captured this useless gesture of solidarity.

Out of the corner of my eye, I catch sight of the lapis lazuli earrings, rain sticks, pig leather wallets, tiny fishing boats with nets, all displayed on the sidewalk. These artisans remind me of some of my Canadian friends with their rebellious hair and colourful vests, legs crossed, sitting behind their work.

I turn the corner in a rush and go into the café, feeling dirty, sticky, and beat with exhaustion. Any moment now, Mireya will materialize at the door, her hair all over the place, Mapuche bag across her chest, double C bra with a zipper in front that twenty years ago was like a poncho on me but fit her just fine, granny shoes, fingernails covered with paint, and letting loose a peal of laughter, displaying a row of even white teeth.

I savour a large cappuccino with my eyes on the door. I hardly notice the arrival of a woman in her forties dressed like a hippie: grey hair to her shoulders, tons of bracelets tinkling on her wrist, hands stained with colour. The unmistakable laughter revealing a not-so-white row of teeth shakes me up and I jump from my chair like a spring. I throw myself on her ample bosom and plunge into her warmth, into twenty years of absences, a whole life of absences; into Mireya's strength, into her sobs. Life has not treated us so badly, she says, as she looks me up and down, warm tears running down her face. And then I get an uncontrollable desire to laugh and since Mireya laughs at the drop of a hat, in no time she is laughing with me and we laugh and laugh and laugh like crazy in front of all the customers of The House in The Air, because obviously the military did not count on this good memory, this love: they did not count on this immense desire to live, this propensity to laughter.

Let's go, we have a lot to do, Mireya says, as she grabs my bag with one hand and my arm with the other. What do you think about this plan: we go home to El Arrayán, put on some Mercedes Sosa, our favourite, or Rubén Blades (who, by the way, did not exist twenty years ago, don't you love his music?), and eat a lasagna like the one we made that terrible night I stayed at your place because we thought the military would come for you and you didn't want the girls and your mother to be alone, so we made the dough with chopped fresh basil leaves in it and since we didn't have any ground beef for the sauce, we killed one of the girls' chickens, we need to have protein and a balanced diet, you said, tomorrow we'll explain it to the girls and when they try the lasagna they'll understand for sure, but they didn't understand shit and cried for hours and we felt guilty as hell, but the lasagna was great and after all the military didn't come, but we had a great time cooking all night. . . .